Diaper Rash . . .

He laughed and sat upright on the edge of the bed.

"You ask too many questions," he said. Then, glancing at her tan bikini, "and you're wearing too many clothes."

"Nonsense."

"Take off that diaper thing."

"No."

"Sheri—please."

Begging came hard to him, she guessed. She said, "I don't feel right, walking around nude in the middle of the day."

"It's not the middle of the day—it's evening."

"I still don't feel right."

He rose slowly and stretched his arms, fit and poised as a giant cat.

"Jim, why do you want someone like me, when you have a wife like Lili?"

He grinned tolerantly. "Let's not talk about her," he said. "I'd rather do something else . . ."

MOTEL WIVES

JAY CARR

MOTEL WIVES

1

AN ENORMOUS SUN was cut in half by the line between sky and ocean. Little by little, the visible part became less than half a sphere. A long sunset glow shimmered across the Pacific and fired a puff of cotton cloud in an untroubled sky.

Kevin Morris slowed his car and enjoyed the splendid moment. This was his favorite time of the twenty-four hour stretch, the instant between day's bustle and the evening's promised excitement.

Once he had shared awareness of the hour. He remembered the hi-fi echoing through the newness of their house, meshing with the tinkle of ice cubes as Felice mixed the first cocktails of evening. He remembered her sensuous laughter shocking him, reaching out to him, pulling at his insides, telling him once again that she was his, his alone—that cool, fresh sheets awaited them in the other room if they could make it that far. Their lovemaking before dinner would be tumultuous and frenetic, almost a battle of survival.

Perhaps, he thought bitterly, that had been the trouble—we made love before dinner, after dinner and during the night. We made love all the time, every time possible. No man could have kept up with her. Now Felice was his no longer. No more Felice. Ever.

A pang of loneliness for her struck him solidly wherever it was he lived, making the sunset's beauty

7

an alien, hostile thing. The steering wheel wavered briefly in his hands. He blinked rapidly, fighting to rid himself of weakness. A car zoomed by him, honking a garish horn.

There was a nagging tiredness in the small of his back. His eyes felt undependable and he knew he had been driving far too long. The distance had not been great but he had started the trip tired. Now suddenly he was drained as though some hungry other being had sucked away his strength.

The highway crested a short hill. Below him and to his right, the land projected into the sea, forming a small ragged peninsula where tall palms waved in the rising breeze. Through the foliage, he could see some red-tiled roofs. A highway sign loomed larger on his right, extending an invitation. DEW DROP INN.

Why not? This seemed as good a place as any. He was fleeing a memory. Where he paused and what he did were matters of no importance. He had left San Francisco that morning, heading vaguely for Los Angeles. He had given himself a week's freedom from his law office. During that week he had to try and cure himself of his horrible self-pity.

But nothing waited for him in Los Angeles, just as there was nothing behind him—not since Felice had left for Reno three months ago—in San Francisco.

He shook his head angrily. He had to quit feeling gypped because he had been unequal to keeping his wife. What man could have done better?

He remembered the psychiatrist's words, the way the calm, gray-haired man had looked at him dispassionately from beyond the desk. "Felice is a nymphomaniac, Kevin," the psychiatrist had said. "With the proper treatment, the proper kind of attitude from you, she can be cured. I know that's a large order."

The memory gave him a bad reaction. He swung

off the main highway to the blacktopped side road leading down to the palms. A figure in white suddenly appeared in front of him. He lurched crazily against the steering wheel, feeling the shimmy as the car swung away from the side of the road.

He glanced in the rear-view mirror. A woman stared after him, hand to her mouth, slim and unmoving in the dusk. He thought to slow down and offer apologies, but found he was in no mood for amenities.

The road dropped and narrowed to a defile in sandy rock, then rose again to a wide plateau that was rather like a parking lot in the desert. Ahead lay a rambling, one-storied stucco building with a red-tiled roof. At varying distances, smaller buildings of similar style stood in random pattern among the palm trees. The grounds seemed carefully kept.

Kevin pulled behind another car and parked. He sat for a moment, hands clenched on the steering wheel, thinking how close he had come to hitting the woman on the road. He shuddered involuntarily. His life lately had been a mess. Involvement in an accident would have added the final touch.

The woman had been beautiful, even in the brief glimpse he had gotten of her. He was out of practice. Beautiful women had not interested him since Felice had put him through the nightmare of her illness. He was unable to look at women now with normal perspective. He saw them all in the light of the agonizing demands that Felice had made of him. He wondered how long he would ignore what was basic within him, the drive of man for woman. Not forever—celibacy to his dying day would have been as insane for Kevin as the wild marital orgy which had preceded divorce. But Felice had drained him emotionally as well as physically. She had led him on a toboggan from ecstasy to hell, to a place where he felt like a play-

9

thing of devils. Not Felice, but her obsession with sex, had become his private hell. They had lost each other in her soulless fever.

He still felt the pull of hunger for a woman—but what woman would ever match the girl he had married and lost?

He pulled himself together and got slowly out of the car. He was tall and solid, just past thirty, with deep-set green-gray eyes and ebony-black hair cropped close to his skull. His tan slacks and white shirt, he thought, probably showed less wear and tear after a day's driving than Kevin did himself. They were making the clothes these days better than they made people.

He could hear splash and laughter from a swimming pool, but the pool was out of sight. A young couple walked slowly across the lawn, holding hands, their bowed heads almost touching, whispering, unaware of the cruel world about them—or possibly within them. He remembered the time of his honeymoon in a place not unlike this one—both naked, he and Felice had stayed in bed for hours on end, gulping at each other, trying to drain every last ounce of energy from each other . . .

He turned at the sound of footsteps. The woman behind him was golden brown from the sun. Her ash-blond air was held back from her brow by a wide pink band. She wore white tennis shorts and a white sleeveless blouse. Her face was almost too beautiful to be real. She stopped and studied Kevin with lively blue eyes before she snapped, "Damn you to hell, stranger."

This was the woman who had made him swerve on the road. He tried to smile. "I'm sorry. I didn't mean to frighten you."

"I saw your face when you drove by. You can't tell

me you were watching the road. First I thought you were drunk."

"I'm not," Kevin said. "I may have driven too many miles today."

"Next time," she said, a little of the anger leaving her voice, "have the decency to stop."

He watched her walk away, idly considering that her words meant more than she probably realized. The decency to stop—decency and a stopping place were exactly what he was looking for. He was not aware of discovery at the time, but he knew that some of the edge had drifted out of his bitterness.

Sheri Carroll sipped at her gin-and-tonic and turned away from the window. She had witnessed the scene in the parking lot and now she was confused.

"Boy," she told Jim Thompson, who was sprawled nakedly on the bed at the far side of the room, "that wife of yours has a temper."

Jim laughed uncomfortably. "That's news? I've lived with her for three years." He looked over the top of his magazine. "What's happening?"

"She just chewed out some tourist down in the parking lot. He didn't have a chance."

Jim said, "I can imagine." He put his magazine down and gave Sheri a long look. The bed was king-sized but he needed all its length. In relaxation, his smooth rippling muscles looked as nerveless as an animal's—or an athlete's. His hair was blond and carefully trimmed, giving him a curious air of being well-dressed though he wore no clothes whatever.

"You're pretty," he said finally. "I suppose you have what they call an elfin beauty. Why are you so distant? Come on over."

"Maybe because I'm suddenly ashamed," Sheri said slowly. She wore only the bottom of a tan linen bikini.

Her breasts were small, high and hard—she liked to think of them as also being proud. "Your wife's a beautiful woman. Why did you come to me, Jim? Why were you so easy to seduce? The wives in my life are hardly ever beautiful—and neither are the men. You're different."

He laughed and sat upright on the edge of the bed.

"You ask too many questions," he said. "And you're wearing too many clothes."

"Nonsense."

"Take off that diaper thing. Let me look at you as you walk to me."

"No."

"Sheri—please."

Begging came hard to him, she guessed. She said, "I don't feel right, walking around nude in the middle of the day."

"It's not the middle of the day—it's evening."

"I still don't feel right." She took another sip of gin-and-tonic. "I'm sorry—but you somehow keep reminding me of a human being. And dammit, I'm embarrassed."

He rose slowly and stretched his arms with a satisfied exhalation, fit and poised as a giant cat. The way he was looking at her reminded her of Sammy, frightened her the way Sammy had always frightened her. She shut the memory quickly out of her mind.

"Jim, I want you to listen," she insisted. "Why do you want someone like me, when you have a wife like Lili? I've never seen a more beautiful woman."

He grinned tolerantly. The grin implied that he and Sheri needed no meeting of minds—that their purpose in being together was to be unmixed with any pretense at understanding or warmth.

"Let's not talk about her," he said. "I'd rather do something else."

If that was the relationship he wanted, he could have it. "We've already had our fun for the day," she pointed out briskly, commercially.

"I want it again."

She took a backward step. "I'm not a machine, Jim," she said.

He laughed and pounced, ripping the brief bikini away from her body. She was conscious of tossing her drink into his face and then his arms were around her, engulfing her. His mouth covered her lips.

The ever-smoldering fire broke within her into dancing flames. She swung her face to one side, biting his bare shoulder. He screamed deep in his throat, loosening his hold. She slipped away.

"Don't force it, Jim," she whispered. "I don't like to be forced." She was breathing deeply, her breasts rising and falling in an uneven rhythm. "When I want it, I'll let you know."

He hesitated. "Don't tease me," he warned.

She watched him with fascination, no longer able to shut memories out of her mind. What was there about her that drew men like Jim Thompson—like Sammy? They seemed to know at a glance, as though they smelled the fact, that she could be theirs for the asking. But none of them ever were hers. Some of the men she had known had wanted more than a one-night stand. She had had offers of marriage, some of which a more practical whore would have grabbed at. In fact, even a good girl, to use the vulgar expression, might have thought twice about turning down at least one of her offers.

No offer had ever come from someone Sheri wanted to know any better.

2

SOME DAY, SHERI told herself, a man she really wanted to know would want to know Sheri. And if she could be wise enough, maybe this was the day.

She continued watching Jim. He kept his hand on his shoulder where she had bitten him and his eyes had a dark sheen. Suddenly and helplessly, she wanted him so much that she had to fight for control. Their lovemaking earlier had only hinted at glory. The instant somehow had been too brief, over too quickly. What she wanted now was a slow and sensuous experience. She wanted to know him and to be known by him, to learn why he was here with her instead of with his wife.

"Sit down on the bed," she ordered.

He hesitated, the dark sheen still in his eyes. He was angry and she liked it. His kind got what they wanted. She knew he was seething inwardly at last.

She stroked her little breasts, fondling them in front of him, fingering the nipples between her forefinger and thumb.

"You like?" she asked.

He groaned in a shock of appreciation.

"Sit down, Jim," she ordered again.

He slumped back on the bed. "Come here." He did not know he was begging. Not yet.

"In due time, darling," she said.

She walked in front of him, accentuating the wiggle of her hips, rolling them forward, watching his eyes, watching the way they lit up with anticipation as she approached him. And then she stopped in her tracks.

"I want to know," she said, "why you're here with me and not with your wife."

He did not answer.

"Okay," she said, turning away from him, fighting the passion within her.

He sprang from the bed, clutched her wrist and made her face him again.

"Not that it's your business," he said. "But Lili's a cold fish. She doesn't give a damn about men."

"All men, or just you?"

"Who knows?" he answered. "Maybe she finds me particularly repulsive."

"And me, Jim? What about me?"

"The first time I saw you yesterday at the pool—the wiggle of your cute little fanny as you paraded by—I swore I'd get into bed with you. You got me hot just watching you walk."

She had practiced that walk many times. She was pleased by what he had said. She put her palms to his cheeks, pulled his face against her body. She shivered ecstatically at the hunger of his lips.

And then he lay on his back and she threw herself against him, knowing that she was yielding partly to the man but more to her own boundless taste for physical pleasure. He had given her the scantest fragment of insight into the inner world that was himself—and she accepted the fragment, cheap woman that she was, in exchange for all she could give. She marveled at herself as she moaned and writhed with his mastering lust.

Lili Thompson finished brushing her hair and stepped back from the mirror, frowning at her reflection. In the bra and panties she wore, she thought, she looked absurdly and sternly healthy, like a girl on a poster promoting a physical fitness program.

She walked to the window, reaching for the drawstring to close the drapes. Preceded by a bellhop, a man passed on the walk outside. She recognized the motorist who had just missed hitting her on the road. He turned his head and their eyes met before the drapes fell shut.

She felt her cheeks flush, though not with shame. She leaned her head against the cool wall, closing her eyes, fighting a sense of loneliness. She stood her ground for a long moment, then abruptly moved to the closet on the far side of the bed. The dress she chose after impatient searching was pale pink cotton with short sleeves.

Where was Jim? She realized she was hoping that she did not know the answer, made herself admit her almost certain knowledge. He had had his eye on that little vagrant, Sheri, ever since yesterday afternoon. If he was not with her now, he would be soon. Good old Jim never wasted more time than he had to. She felt sudden corrosive anger. The tears came against her will. She stumbled against the edge of the bed and sat down to collect herself.

She had counted on this vacation to work out all the problems between her and Jim during the past year or so. Away from their friends, away from any reminders of the little trying habits that had grown into causes of war for each of them, she had thought they might rekindle some of the love they had shared in the beginning.

But had Jim ever truly loved her? Or had he only wanted to possess her, the way he possessed other people and things?

Whatever, the vacation was not working. Their marriage was the same old story although with a change of scene. Remembering the violence of their

16

argument the night before, she shuddered. His tongue had been vile. He had called her filthy names.

What did he expect? How could she make physical love to him, knowing what she did? In the beginning, he had seemed to her a knight in stainless armor, strong and virtuous, a man assured of success with no further effort than being true to himself. He had been —still was—rising in banking and investments. Prizes came easily to Jim, as though by natural attraction.

Had some of the fault for the failure of their marriage been hers? The first year had been wonderful. Living with a man, having him whenever she wanted him, letting herself go and being his woman, had been an incredible release for her, though somewhat against the grain.

But the bloom had faded. They had grown apart. He was not the man she had imagined. She had seen the chinks in his armor, the little fears and falsehoods that added up to the fact that he was a fake. Ironically, Lili was the one person whom he seldom fooled. But in learning his duplicity, she had lost her hero. The knowledge of what he was had chilled her emotions toward him.

She could no longer enjoy their lovemaking. She hardly even bothered pretending any more. The pleasure of sex had become a chore, a duty to be gotten through as quickly as possible, if only to get his body away from hers.

She supposed the rift had started back when she had discovered him with Sally—a nonentity, perhaps a call girl brought by a business associate—at the beach party, the two of them tucked behind a rise in the sand like a couple of animals. Others had followed Sally, how many she did not know. The actual number made no difference. One was as bad as a hundred.

She still had not pulled the dress over her head. She had bought the pink cotton to please him. Jim liked her in pink. She felt the tears again.

She had to get hold of herself, take a grip on her feelings. She was not the kind to weep. Who knew better than she that marriages could flop? Her own parents had made a mess of their lives. As far back as she could remember, they had bickered and argued and figured ways of punishing one another, though for what, Lili never was sure.

Lonely and miserable, listening to the quarrels, she had made up her mind that her own marriage would be different. No matter what happened, she had promised herself in childhood and adolescence, she would be forgiving and kind.

She had not reckoned with sex—that inescapably honest act which told you when you were furious, no matter how kind and forgiving you pretended to be.

She rose, preparing to slip the dress on. The door opened and Jim came in, a tight little smirk of conquest at the corner of his mouth.

She slipped the dress over her head, then asked, "Is there any sense in your telling me where you've been?"

"Out," was all he replied.

She stifled her instantly growing anger. "Are you having dinner with me, Jim?"

He relaxed into an orange-colored chair and took his time about lighting a cigarette.

"Of course," he answered finally.

"Was she good?" She had not meant to ask that.

"I'm not sure I understand." His face was a handsome mask that told her nothing. There was still time to avoid a quarrel—to maintain peace if not affection between them.

"All right," she said slowly. "Have it your way. You always do."

18

"What's that supposed to mean?"

She busied herself in front of the dresser mirror, putting on lipstick, letting her sudden silence set the tone for the evening.

Once again, he had spoiled everything. She had hoped this vacation would be different, that he would at least give their relationship a try. His wife should have been worth that much to him.

"Lili," he said, "I thought we were going to stop this bickering, these suspicions of yours."

So that was what he had thought—that Lili was the one who needed reform.

"Let's not discuss it," she said sharply.

"Is that what you really mean?"

She turned to face him. As always these days, his exceptional good looks gave her a pang of jealousy. But neither his looks nor his temperament were his own fault. His mother, she knew, had spoiled him completely, giving him everything he wanted and many woman after her had had the same impulse. Lili, too, had chased him in the beginning, thinking he was the only man for her. She had wanted him and now she had him and was sorry. All she had gained were those precious memories of the first year. Whatever was wrong, that first year had been right and it could not be stolen from her.

"How should I feel?" she asked, knowing the senselessness of her words, old words that she had used before. "I know what you've been doing. I can tell by the look on your face. Don't you think I know that look by now, Jim? I've seen it often enough. Who was it this time? Sheri Carroll? She looks like the kind who—"

"You've got a damned unkind nature, Lili," he interrupted.

She laughed harshly. "You're actually funny in a way," she said. "You can sit there and criticize me as though I were the one at fault. Why do you think I've got a suspicious, unkind nature? Don't you think you've given me cause?"

"Oh, hell," he snapped. "Let's not talk."

She snapped back at him. "Let's not face the truth, you mean. The truth hurts, doesn't it, Jim? You're a big, handsome son-of-a-bitch, and you can't help it if every woman gets amorous for you, can you? Well, here's one woman who's fed up. I've had it, right up to here—" she indicated her chin "—and you might as well know it now."

He yawned maddeningly. "What does that mean?"

"What do you think it means?" She tried to conquer her anger and failed. "What will the partners think at the bank when it comes out in divorce court what a first-class bastard you are?"

His face was suddenly harsh and drawn in the dim light. "You've always had a habit of blaming me," he said without spirit, "and now you're threatening me. Okay. Go as far as you want with your threat. Sure, I was with Sheri. I was with her all afternoon and I made love to her twice, if you want to make it your business. We had a good time. I'm a man and she's a woman and she was sure as hell in favor of the difference." His tone changed subtly from one of defeat to the wheedling half-whisper she knew so well. "What am I supposed to do, Lili? I look at that gorgeous body of yours and I want you like crazy. When I have you, what good does it do me? Absolutely none. You don't think you kid me, do you? You're cold to me, Lili. We both know that. I look down in your eyes when we ought to be one person and I can see that you're not with me, that you don't give a damn what I'm doing, that I'm not good enough for you. You're just going through the motions."

"Was it always that way, Jim?" she asked with desperate calm.

"No," he answered slowly. "You once liked me, Lili—or imagined that you liked me. Maybe you've never known me. I think the man you liked was a myth with my face and name. You cheated on me with him."

She gasped, "And you say I blame you for everything. Maybe I have to blame you in self-defense. Which one of us really cheats? Which one started a year ago with a little bitch on the beach? Whenever you make love to me now, I wonder just as you do if it's really me you're loving, or just any woman who gives herself to you."

"Lili, let's—"

She was no longer listening. She stamped across the room, slamming the door behind her.

Shaking with anger and frustration, she moved along the walk, conscious of laughter from the cabin next door. Full night had come and light from the cabin windows splashed before her along the walk. The palms waved eerily above, gigantic watching ghosts whose intent, whether good or evil, she could not guess.

She walked to the small grassy area that overlooked the beach. A campfire flickered below her on the sand. Soft voices reached her ears. The night wind touched her bare arms. She wished she had brought a sweater.

Was Jim even partly right—was some of the fault hers for the sickness of their marriage? He had behaved badly tonight. He had not even defended himself for indefensible conduct. Instead—of all the crazy things—he had twisted things around to accuse Lili of cheating.

She no longer fought the tears.

She knew for whom her tears were shed. Like a widow, she mourned the man she had loved and lost—

the man with whom Jim had accused her of cheating on him.

The man was Jim as she had imagined him when they first were married.

A chivalrous man.

Her parents had been strict about her choice of friends, had occasionally hurt her feelings by too plainly disapproving of some guest she might bring home.

Jim had always gotten along with her friends.

She had had a classmate named Aggie Moore, a dark-eyed modified beatnik with whom she could share a good healthy intellectual argument of the kind you cherished while you were still in college.

Her parents had been all but downright rude to Aggie. Aggie had forgiven them. "Your folks," she had told Lili, "are dedicated to all that is mediocre. They are starry-eyed nobodies. They are fanatic conformists and I make allowances for fanatics. You must do the same."

Lili had been unable to share Aggie's tolerant attitude, had resented her mother's suggestion, made in front of Aggie, that Aggie needed a bath.

Jim, on the other hand, had been wonderful to Aggie.

"Any friend of my wife's," he had said, "is a friend of mine."

During the first year of her marriage, Lili had glowed at the happy change in Aggie.

"Now that she feels welcome in someone's nice home," Lili had praised Jim for his kindness, "she looks actually pretty. You've been an angel. Introducing her to your friends, telling her when you like her dress—come to think of it, I used to think she didn't even own a dress."

Jim had given her what she thought a mock-leer.

"That's me," he'd agreed. "The twentieth century's gift to women. Don't you ever get jealous?"

She had laughed and kissed him possessively.

Many months later she had learned that she had cause for jealousy. By then she had learned so much besides that Aggie Moore's treachery was a mere drop in the bucket.

Even after she learned there were other women, the hero myth had lingered. Weeping, she had said to Jim, "I won't stand in your way if she's the one you love. I'll always be proud of having been your wife."

"Don't leave me," he had asked. "You're the one I love."

She had mistaken his tomcatting for some larger human emotion.

She no longer even thought of him as being unfaithful to her. She would have minded less if he had fallen in love with someone else.

She no longer thought he was capable of love. To Jim, sex was a different kind of martini, nothing more.

She felt degraded for having been his partner.

And the degradation of course would have to go on and on. She wondered if some day she would become like Jim, callous to anyone else's sensitivities, predatory—

In short, a bum.

She had already noted a certain grimness in herself that was frightening. When she met new people, she tended to be suspicious, hostile. Sometimes, compensating for the tendency, she had to stop herself from being too friendly, too meddlesome.

There seemed no escape from the trap of unhappiness her marriage was weaving around her—every attempt at freedom only snarled the knots more hopelessly.

3

KEVIN SAT AT the bar with his half-finished martini, listening to the voices of people who had each other.

The young couple he had glimpsed earlier that day was huddled at a table in the far corner, oblivious to the world. Not too long ago, Kevin and Felice had been like that.

He had to stop thinking of Felice.

He sipped the martini. He had registered at the motel here, showered, shaved and changed his clothes, in an effort to rejoin the human race. He liked the calm tempo of this spot, the comfort of his cabin, the absence of drummed-up excitement or professional entertainment. He wanted to put all thoughts of the immediate past from his mind—or at least to try.

The bartender mopped the already dry bar in front of him. "Another one, sir?"

Kevin shook his head. "Later." Feeling the need to talk to someone, anyone, he continued, "Nice place."

"We get a good crowd most of the time," the bartender said. He was a wiry little man, small enough to be a jockey, with eyes that were almost too bright a blue. "You alone, sir?"

"Yes."

"That's the way I like my own vacations. Yessir. My wife and me, we always take separate vacations. Better that way. Last year I spent two weeks in a Hollywood hotel, all alone. I slept and slept and went out to Hollywood Park every day and tried to beat the horses."

"Did you beat them?"

The little man laughed. "You kidding? Who ever does?"

"I guess no one," Kevin said.

The bartender leaned forward, his elbows resting on the rim of the bar. "Mildred—that's my wife—she thinks I'm cheating on her during my vacations. But I really don't. Did once, three years ago, and I couldn't sleep for a week afterwards, thinking about it."

"How about her?"

The blue eyes danced. "That's her business. For fifty weeks of the year, she's a damned good wife, looks after me and my wishes and I've got no gripes."

"More of us should have that philosophy," Kevin said.

"Maybe. There's a lot of cheating goes on around a place like this, believe me, and people get upset all the time. So what, I always say."

A haughty little waitress called the bartender and, having expounded his philosophy, he moved away.

Glancing around the small bar, Kevin noted that he was the only person present who had no companion. He had a helpless sense of embarrassment and jealousy, such as he had not known since he had been in college. He thought of getting drunk, dismissed the thought. He did not enjoy drunkenness.

In spite of himself, he brooded. What had gone wrong with Felice? The psychiatrist had given him nothing he could live by. The situation obsessed him and, try as he might, he could not resolve it within his own mind.

He was getting ready to order another martini when he recognized the woman who was entering the bar.

She was wearing a pale pink dress that clung sensuously to the fine lines of her body. Her hair was slightly wind-blown. A frown marred the beauty of her face. She stood in the small entryway as if uncertain which way to turn, whether to head for the bar on her right or the dining room on her left. She did not seem the kind of woman who would be confused about so trivial a decision. Perhaps she was looking for someone.

She entered the bar and took a corner table near the young lovers. Kevin watched her seat herself, her thigh muscles taut and smooth against the dress. He remembered how she had looked earlier in shorts.

The waitress took her order and relayed it to the bar.

He still owed her an apology, Kevin reasoned. Two apologies, if he counted the glimpse he had had of her at the window in her undies. He smiled at the memory. If anything, she had looked sterner in lingerie than in sport clothes. He could not have approached a woman who had the same kind of ravishing beauty that Felice had possessed. The lady in the corner was beautiful too—but in a reassuringly chilly way that matched his own unhappiness.

He rose and walked toward her. She lifted her face at his approach and he saw the burning anger in her eyes. He did not think the anger was for him.

"I would like to apologize again," he said. "This time, for being ungracious."

She did not answer. He noted a slight puffiness around her eyes. She had been crying. She was lost and unhappy, like himself. The knowledge pleased him, took away some of his loneliness.

"May I sit down?" he asked.

"Why?"

The abruptness of her question surprised him. He

answered frankly, "Because you're the only other person alone in this room."

"At least you're honest."

"One of my shortcomings."

"Has it anything to do with the way you saw me in the window?"

Again she had surprised him.

"Yes," he said. "You might as well have been wearing armor, in case you felt embarrassed. I thought you'd like to know."

Her expression changed to something he could not read. He wondered suddenly if he were acting wisely. The waitress returned with the lady's drink and set it on the table, giving Kevin a pert little smile which meant he could try her later.

The woman's wedding ring flashed as she reached for her drink. "All right," she said. "Sit down, if you wish."

He sat. "You had every right to be angry," he said. "My mind was a long way off this afternoon. I shouldn't even have been driving under the circumstances."

"I couldn't agree with you more."

"And the other—that was an accident. I just happened to turn my head and there you were."

"I don't usually stand half-dressed before an open window."

"I imagine not." He paused. "Are you always angry?"

She gave him a surprised look, then shook her head.

"This hasn't been one of my better days," she explained slowly, almost apologetically.

"We all have them."

"I suppose it's a sign of the times. Like these." She raised her martini. "One almost has to drink martinis now to belong."

"Belong to what?"

For the first time, she noticed that Kevin had no drink in front of him—he still had not ordered the second martini.

"I don't know," she said. She glanced at the young couple at the next table. They had been whispering together. The girl giggled and nuzzled her lover's ear playfully. The young man's hand was under the table.

"They're happy, at least," the woman in pink said bitterly.

Kevin made no comment. He had problems of his own and her bitterness was something he could do without.

"I'm the one who should apologize now," she said. "I'm afraid I'm not good company. If you'd like to go back to the bar and leave me alone, I'll understand."

He was half tempted to accept the out offering. For whatever reason, she was at war with herself and the battle did not concern him. He looked at her carefully, at full proud lips and wide brow, and felt suddenly protective.

"Look," he heard himself saying, "let's start again. We've both made our apologies. Let's leave it at that." He smiled. "The world can't be that bad for either of us."

"Can't it?" she asked and then she smiled. "Wow. I certainly seem to be taking myself seriously. This is supposed to be a vacation and I'm supposed to be having a good time, not spreading gloom. I've been here for two days, soaking up the sun, swimming, walking—but I guess I forgot to laugh at myself."

He looked at her wedding ring. "Are you alone?" he asked.

She shook her head.

He felt amused by his own disappointment. What had he expected? This woman was not the kind who would be cheating on her husband—except that appearances were deceptive. Felice had not looked like a bum and yet she had been one. She had taken any and every man she could find and, regardless of what the psychiatrist had said about her sickness, Kevin could not justify her actions to himself.

"You're too beautiful to be sad and angry," he said. He noticed that her drink was finished and motioned for service, finally ordering his own martini and a refill for his companion. She took the cigarette he offered and he held the match for both of them.

"I suppose you're wondering about me," she said. "I'm a married woman, here with my husband, yet I'm allowing a perfect stranger to buy me a drink."

"Where is your husband now?"

"I—he was in the cabin when I left."

"I hope he isn't big and mean and jealous," Kevin said, trying to smile.

"He's never had reason to be jealous." Her face turned softer. "He's big, though, and he can be mean at times. So if you're frightened—" She let the sentence trail.

"You seem to want to get rid of me."

"I don't know that yet," she said.

"I don't even know your name. Mine's Kevin."

She hesitated as the waitress returned with their drinks. Then she said, "Lili."

He raised his glass in a toast. "Here's to all the unhappy people."

"I guess I'm not the only bitter one at this table," she said. "You're married too, aren't you, Kevin?"

"I—was."

"Divorced?"

He nodded silently. The word took getting used to.

"What's it like to live with someone for a long time, sharing your life, and then—" Again she left her sentence unfinished.

29

"The truth is that it's horrible, pure hell," Kevin said.

"You're still in love with her." Lili was making a statement, not asking a question.

"I guess I am, in a way."

She leaned forward, studying his face intently. "Please don't get the wrong idea. I feel like getting out of here, walking against the night wind in my face. Come with me if you like."

He nodded, rose and moved behind her to pull out her chair. As he followed Lili toward the doorway, the little bartender caught his eye and winked obscenely.

Before they left the building, the door swung inward. A big, good-looking blond man stopped short in their path. He seemed startled at the sight of them together.

"Hello, Jim," Lili said evenly. "This is my friend, Kevin. Kevin, meet my husband."

Jim ignored the introduction. "Where do you think you're going?" he asked Lili.

"Does it make any difference?" Lili turned to Kevin, her eyes begging for understanding. She said, "Are you coming with me?"

"If you wish," he answered quickly, knowing he was a fool to get involved in a family squabble, yet not giving a damn.

As a lawyer, he knew perhaps better than the average person that to come between husband and wife, especially when the two were not getting along, was a form of self-destruction.

Perhaps, he thought with wry humor, this would be his solution to the mess of life. He had loused up his own affairs with a bad marriage—by helping to compound another bad marriage, he might straighten things out for keeps.

He recalled a client who had actually faced a prison term, the direct result of trying to understand someone else's wife. Understanding had involved, finally, embezzlement of funds. The lady, scarred psychically by life's blows, had required a vacation in Hawaii to restore her peace of mind.

Be a sucker, Kevin told himself. Be a chump. Throw yourself away. He had always been careful to follow rational plans—and look at him now.

There was just one drawback.

The world had trouble-prone people in it, exciting characters who accounted for most of history. Nine-tenths of all lawsuits happened to them, two-thirds of all accidents, and more than their fair share of bad domestic crises.

Others, less conspicuous, were as inescapably doomed to stay out of trouble.

On the one day in five years when they were late for trains, the trains would also run late. Bombs exploded in places they had not yet reached. When a trouble-proof man threw all restraint to the winds and scraped up acquaintance with a strange girl at a bar, she usually turned out to be as solid as he was.

What a joke—if both he and the ash blonde were congenitally trouble-proof.

What a lousy, bitter joke.

4

KEVIN BRUSHED PAST Jim Thompson to follow Lili outside. The night wind from the ocean was cold against his face. He turned for a backward look, almost expecting to see her husband. But the blond man did not come. Lili's laughter was softer than wind or surf.

"The shoe's on the other foot," she said.

She had walked ahead, away from the lights of the building, and he hurried to catch up, wondering what kind of mess he had gotten himself into, perversely hoping for trouble enough to escape his own problems. What did he have to lose?

They came to a small, steep path that led down to the beach. Lili paused to remove her high-heeled shoes. A shoe in each hand, she continued down the path. Kevin followed.

The wind was stiffer on the beach. The darkness was real down here, deep and black and unfathomable. For a moment there was sudden light. He looked up. Clouds had blown away from the face of the moon. Lili and he were spotlighted for the whole watching sky—only for a moment. Then utter darkness descended on them again.

He trudged beside her across the sand, bemused as though in a dream. Down here the surf was loud, drowning out the sense of whatever she was trying to say. He knew she was speaking, but he could not make out the words.

She turned to face him near the water's edge. Again he tried to make out what she was saying but the words stopped mattering. They had reached a world where no one else existed, where there were the two of them and their loneliness and the sea.

She moved against him and he put his arms around her, feeling the soft silkiness of her hair against his mouth. Her lips touched his throat. She moved back to look at him in the dimness. Now she was close enough for her words to be clear. She asked, "Tell me again, Kevin. Tell me I'm too beautiful to be sad."

"You're beautiful, Lili."

"Again."

"You're beautiful."

The lines and curves of her body molded to his own. A surge of passion swept him, devastating in its intensity.

"Do you want me, Kevin?"

For answer, his mouth closed on hers, harshly and demandingly. Their lips clung together, moved bruisingly. He was lost in a passion that was like the sea. Dimly he was aware of removing his own clothing, of seeing her white nakedness. Lili became a nymph from the western ocean . . .

She was beside him in the sand, her thighs fiercely around him, her mouth searching for his with undeniable lust. The grinding sand tore at his knees but he was unmindful of hurt, knowing only the rhythm of desire. The pounding of surf, the pounding of his blood and Lili's, became one. The incoming waves washed against their feet. With each wave, he was pushed farther and farther into the deep well of desire. Then the universe exploded and he felt her shudder beneath him and a sudden, awesome quiet.

He turned on his back, cold, shivering, at peace with himself for the first time in longer than he could

33

remember. It was good to know that he could still want a woman.

She said, "I'm sorry, Kevin," and her voice was a long way off.

Not understanding, he turned to her, wanting to hold her once again, but she rose to her feet and stood above him, a pale, blurred shape in the darkness.

"Lili?" he pleaded.

"No, Kevin," she said. With her clothing in her arms, she turned and ran from him.

Lili ran until her legs ached and her lungs gasped in protest. She collapsed to her knees on the sand, still clutching her clothing.

The surf seemed to match the tumult of her soul. She was a bad woman. She had had a lover. Nothing would ever blot out the fact. She had enjoyed her transgression. She had never known, not even in the beginning with Jim, that sex could be an earth-shattering experience.

She made no effort to hide her guilt from herself. She was a married woman. She had picked up a stranger in a bar and let him make love to her. If she prettied the truth to herself, she might lose not only virtue but sanity.

She looked down the beach into the impenetrable night, wondering if Kevin had tried to follow her. She also wondered what he thought of her—probably what any man would think. She had acted like any common whore, no better and no worse.

She suddenly remembered the burning touch of his strong yet gentle hands against her body, the way his mouth had worked against her own, building the lust within her into a rising crescendo, the long-forgotten lust that Jim had pushed aside. Perhaps by now in

34

his thoughts the stranger considered her trash—but he had not despised her with his body. Slowly, she rose to her feet, stifling an impulse to go back to him.

He had tried to be kind to her in the bar, to talk to her and help her. She should have been grateful and let it go at that. Had she used him to get even with her husband?

She still had not put on her clothing. In a gesture she barely understood, she balled up her panties and bra, rolled them in damp sand and threw them as far as she could into the water. She slipped into her dress and thought of her shoes.

She had left them at the scene of her transgression. She decided against going back to look for the shoes— to do so would have been an effort to hide her guilt.

Let them lie on the beach, wherever they were, showing where she had forsaken the path of virtue. She recognized her deed as a dangerous one, compounded as it was of acceptance and recklessness. She needed an hour or so alone—she had never lacked for solitude, as Jim's wife, but tonight for the first time she felt grateful to whatever woman was keeping him right now.

Sheri?

She walked up the beach toward the place of light and music where people were making trouble for each other. At least, she thought thankfully, she was bringing with her a portion of darkness and silence from the beach.

When she opened the cabin door, she saw Jim was waiting for her.

Her private silent darkness, she sensed with a certain terror, was about to be assailed.

Jim rose from the contour chair. His face was ugly, a curious phenomenon in a man as handsome as Jim.

The liquor bottle beside the chair was three-fourths empty.

She closed the door behind her and faced his look of fury.

"Where in hell have you been?" he asked.

She could lie to him, she thought, to save herself from his anger, and be safe to go on bickering as they had done before. Their marriage was one long quarrel —but marriages, people said, were supposed to be saved.

"I don't like your tone," she said stiffly. "Ask me again in a pleasant way."

She had no chance to defend herself against his sudden attack. He leaped across the room and slapped her cheek. The blow spun her along the wall. She stumbled against a desk, a shock of pain lashing her body. Instinctively she put her arms in front of her face. But no additional blows were forthcoming.

"When I ask you something, Lili," he said, slowly, bitterly, controlling his voice with seemingly great effort, "I expect you to answer me. Do you understand that? Now I want to know where you were."

"What difference does it make to you? You haven't cared in a long time where I was."

This time, she caught the slap on her upraised arms. The hurt seemed to numb her all the way up to her shoulders.

"Jim," she said, stumbling back, "this won't do you any good." She lowered her arms, faced him squarely. "You can beat me till I'm dead and what will that make you—a husband or a killer?"

"What kind of a woman are you?" he yelled. "You're cold as hell with me and then you run out and pick up some slob in a bar—Lili, I don't understand you."

"I used to want you to understand. Now it doesn't matter."

"Did you—"

"We went for a walk on the beach."

"Was that all?" His face was almost white.

She braced herself. "Of course not."

"You mean you admit it?"

"Of course I admit it. I'm scared of you, Jim. But I'm lots more scared of lying."

He growled like a wild animal, reaching for her. She tried to avoid him but could not. He caught the front of her dress and ripped it away from her body. He yelled something wordless. She slithered away from him. The look in his eyes was insane.

After a while, he managed, "Where're the rest of your clothes?"

"I threw them away," she said. She added, "You ugly man. You lying, ugly man."

5

His fist caught her below the left breast. The air went out of her like a flattened tire. She was dimly aware of falling.

When the black began to subside, her whole body sang out its painful refusal to budge an inch. Finally, she succeeded in reaching the edge of the bed with one hand, turning into a half-sitting position to look at Jim.

He was finishing his liquor with a long swig. He threw the bottle to one side and looked down at her.

"You're filth," he said.

"We're both filth."

"The next time," he said threateningly, "I won't be so easy on you, my beautiful whore of a wife. The next time, I'll kill you. Do you think you can remember that?"

She nodded.

"I'm going out now," he said, "to find me a real woman, not one like you. You sleep on this, Lili. Tomorrow morning, when I come back, I want you to look at me and know what I am and what you are. The next time I touch you, you'll know what I expect."

He walked ponderously away from her, slamming the door behind him as he left.

She sat still for a long time, letting her strength return. In a way, she was thankful for the beating he had given her. Now she owed him nothing. She had evened the score of his cheating and he had found a new way to hurt her. And perhaps the worst hurt of all had been her violation of her own standards with the episode on the beach. She felt no regrets, however. She would never let Jim make love to her again. He might kill her if he wished but that would be the district attorney's worry, not Lili's. She and Jim were finished.

She felt a dull loathing for him.

Sheri sat alone in the barroom's darkest corner, at a tiny table for two. Curiously, although she hated to drink alone, she had spent a great deal of time alone in bars as far back as she could remember. Right now, she was fighting the anger that was building within her. Few things made her angry—she prided herself on her even disposition—but being made to wait for someone else was one of those things.

She glanced at the expensive gold watch on her wrist. Ten-twenty. That bastard Jim had promised to meet her here at ten. He was probably with that gorgeous wife of his. She, Sheri, was good for one thing only. They all ran back to their wives sooner or later, never accepting her tenderness after enjoying her body.

She sighed, closing her eyes. For a moment, she wished she were elsewhere. But no one, she reminded herself, ought to be homesick for hell. Deliberately, she conjured up a frightening memory of Sammy's face dark with anger, the force of his hands as he struck her again and again; but only where it would not show when she was dressed.

Would he try to follow her? She had run out on him feeling sick of the rotten mess that her life had become, sick of doing as he told her all the time, sick of going to bed with fat old men, men too fat to excite her even after she lost the capacity for disgust. They had had a stinking racket, she and Sammy, and she was glad she had run away from him.

But how far had she managed to run?

What was she doing now?

The same old thing—maybe with a slightly different twist. She was still headed in the same direction.

She had sized up the men here at this travelers' oasis, unable to see them in any but Sammy's fashion. He had had that knack of picking out the right ones for plucking, those who would not go screaming about badger game to the cops. In a way, she supposed, she missed the hectic rewards of their life. They had gone only to the best resorts—Las Vegas, Sun Valley, Acapulco.

But did she miss Sammy?

To hell with him.

She could work as well on her own, maybe not as profitably but she still could make a living and keep more for herself. She had what most men wanted, as long as she was careful about picking the right men. Jim Thompson was right, despite being so damned handsome and having that beautiful wife. The rift between Jim and Lili had been obvious to her from her first encounter with them.

She had teased Jim deliberately, a game at which she was expert. She had made discreet inquiries around the motel, discovered that Jim was in banking. Fine, dandy. He would have money enough to interest her. Maybe even—well, maybe it was time she settled down, looked for someone like Jim for more than a weekend. Maybe.

This afternoon she had forgotten about money, forgotten about everything but the pure joy of being with a real man. She had grown used to the unpleasant partners that Sammy had picked for her—the

40

"safe" ones as he called them. Jim was probably not safe. But merely remembering the afternoon sent a warm tingle through her body.

She looked up. Jim was coming through the doorway and she remembered that she had been angry because he had kept her waiting. His face wore an ugly scowl, a fact that pleased her. He had probably been arguing with his wife. Good. The last of her own anger vanished.

He spotted her and came toward her table quickly.

"Don't say anything, darling," she urged, even before he sat down. "From the look on your face, you're mad at the world. Don't you cry on my shoulder because your wife doesn't understand you—let's have a nice time."

His look was one of pure malevolence. "The bitch," he said.

She put a hand on his arm. "Take it easy, Jim. Calm down."

"Let's get out of here," he rasped. She realized that he was on a murderous drunk.

"I'm not leaving until you've calmed down," she said.

He had half-risen from his chair. Her words seemed to penetrate. He sat down again slowly. Sheri's drink stood in front of her, half-finished. He reached for it, draining the glass in one gulp.

His row with his wife must have been a king-sized one. She wondered if she, Sheri, were the cause—if so, she might have to modify her plans.

She turned her head, kissing him lightly on the cheek. The harshness abated in his eyes. He almost smiled.

"Come on now," she whispered, "nothing can be that bad."

"You don't know. You can't possibly know."

"Let's have a drink," she suggested.

He did not bother answering.

She motioned at the waitress, ordered two drinks. Soft music drifted from the dining room next door. There would be dancing, she knew, and she suddenly wanted to dance with him, to rub herself against him, to feel his desire building up. She could take her time with this one, let it last a few days, get all the enjoyment out of him that she could before she tossed her bombshell.

A stray, recurrent thought brought a return of fright. *What if Sammy followed her here?* He had once talked of this place. He would disapprove of her running out on him—strongly. In fact, if he found her, he might damned well kill her.

Jim's hands were busy under the table as the waitress returned with their drinks. She could feel his strength as he squeezed her thigh. He was in a hurry. She parted her legs slightly, carefully watching his face. He flushed. His hand moved up her leg, touched gently and moved away again. His fingertips had set her on fire and she pushed her legs together again. She had never felt like this with a man before.

Not now, she thought. Not now. I have to be careful.

"Didn't you get enough this afternoon?" she asked.

"Never enough," he mumbled.

"Drink your drink, Jim."

He began to look angry again. "Let's—"

"I don't want to be hurried, Jim. You should understand. I like it slow and easy, all the time in the world." She laughed. "No fuss and no muss."

He grinned harmlessly. "Okay. You're the boss."

"That's better, big man."

He laughed aloud, his tension easing again. He gulped his drink, his big hands not too steady. She wondered how much he had had before this meeting. No matter—he had left a beautiful wife to sit in

Sheri's dark corner. She was immensely pleased. Her vanity, often damaged, was comforted and nourished.

He continued to sit quietly, listening to the music with that pointless grin on his face. She realized he was in no mood to dance. Time enough later for dancing, she thought.

They smoked many cigarettes. After a while she said, "Okay, honey, let's have ourselves a ball."

"You mean it?" He was like an eager kid.

"I never say anything I don't mean." She ran the tip of her tongue along her lips. "I've got something special for you this time, honey. Something you'll never forget."

She was burning up inside as she walked with him. This time, she could enjoy it.

She would worry about tomorrow when it came.

But the memory of Sammy was a dark, chilly current in the sea of her fevered lust.

She guessed she didn't really want to forget him. She didn't want him around in person—but she liked the idea that she had known him and learned from him.

He had given her a way of looking at life.

A whole system. He had made her a real person.

6

KEVIN WAS NOT sure that he was awake. He lay un-moving, orienting himself to who he was and where he was and why. He was haunted by a memory of the night—the curious unreality of the lovemaking on the beach.

Had he dreamed the whole incident or had it really happened?

He remembered how beautiful she had been and the warmth of her naked body pulsing and straining against his own. Her eyes had been full of questioning and desire. Had he given the answers she wanted? She had run from him in the end, leaving him puzzled and lonely, and now it was Kevin who felt questioning and desire.

A fly moved across the ceiling, was briefly joined by another. They clung together upside down, defying the laws of gravity. Hands cupped beneath his head, he watched them till they parted and flew away. Last night's episode had been almost that sort of meeting.

But human beings were not like flies, could not touch each other for a moment and then forget.

Last night had to mean more than a mere carnal encounter. The reflection was too familiar. He real-ized with a jolt that he had thought the same way about Felice. When would he learn?

He rolled to his side. Sunlight streamed through the opened drapes, filling the room with hope and warmth. Yesterday morning, he had awakened in his

San Francisco apartment, listless and disinterested. This morning he felt a resurgence of ego and vitality that could not be scoffed away.

Kevin had been raised in a comfortable, middle-class home. He had been given love and understanding. He had liked his parents and most of his high school teachers, reserving a special loyalty for his basketball coach. He took it for granted that he would go to college and law school. He had been considered bright and popular and likely to succeed.

The private world of self that he had brought into marriage with Felice had been perhaps too simple—but he had liked it that way. Now he felt that part of him had been chipped away, leaving a vicious scar.

Felice had burst into his life with that breathtaking beauty of hers that could make a man hear music in the silence. She was gone but the music remained, a chorus of devils' cackles now, mocking him out of the wind. But could he blame her for that? Could anyone be blamed? He had been told that he must not blame her, that she was suffering from a form of mental illness. But, hell, so was he—the illness of being alive and watching while his wife went to bed with any man who would join her.

He had met her at a client's cocktail party at some address he had now forgotten. He had looked into the beauty of her face and known she was for him.

He shuddered and sat up, wondering when his mind would grow scar tissue over Felice and their life together. He would think the hurt was done with and then the memories would start and the distant music that had turned demoniac.

For the first time he saw the shoes. They were narrow and flimsy, a woman's pumps, on the carpet near the doorway. He walked across the room and picked them up, recalling how Lili had run from him.

He did not recall, though, coming back from the beach with her shoes. Who had brought them here, if not himself?

He dropped the shoes to the floor again, shaking his head. He must try to look at last night as an episode with no sequel. Lili was a married woman. Her husband might at this moment be questioning her about last night.

Yet, even as he got out of his pajamas and went into the bathroom for a shower, he could not rid himself of the mood she had evoked. The abrupt cold sting of the water was no help whatever.

He breakfasted alone on black coffee and berries with thick cream, then decided to dispel the memory at the pool.

The pool, a fresh water one, was brilliant in the sunlight. A half dozen people sprawled about on the grass, talking and laughing. A teenage boy was flexing himself at the end of the diving board, but never actually diving. In the water, a man with dark hair and tremendous shoulder muscles was relentlessly doing length after length.

Kevin dropped his towel and entered the shining water. He swam below the surface until he thought his lungs would burst. After getting his breath back he swam ten lengths slowly. Fatigue—it felt like a luxury—developed in his shoulders.

A woman was dangling her feet near the spot where his towel lay. He pulled himself up and out and picked up the towel to dry himself off.

"You're a graceful swimmer," the woman said.

He fluffed the towel through his hair and turned for a better look. The woman was small and trim, with dark, extremely short hair. She was wearing a two-piece suit, pink-dotted on a white background.

"Have a good look," she said without rancor. "I'm used to it."

"I imagine you would be."

"I guess that's meant as a compliment."

"It is," Kevin said.

"Thanks." She moved ever so little, as though making a place.

He sat beside her. From somewhere behind him came a sound of brittle laughter. He had no curiosity about its source.

Th woman's high, firm breasts surprised him. Her diminutive size made her seem almost like a child with a woman's body. Kevin found himself feeling kindly toward her.

"That's better," she said.

"What is?"

"Your smile. I saw you before, walking across the lawn. You had a face like death."

"Maybe I was thinking of death."

Her eyes narrowed. She studied him for a moment, as if trying to make up her mind. She ended by laughing and he laughed with her.

She said, "I like you."

"Everyone likes me."

"I bet you're the life of every party."

"Maybe not every party," he admitted.

He slipped into the water, turned so he could look up at her. Her trailing legs touched his chest in the water.

"Careful, sweetie," she said with too wise a laugh. "I burn easily."

He made a wry face. "I don't like women to call men sweetie," he said.

"Why not?"

"I don't know. It makes me think of greasy dough-nuts and luke-warm coffee."

She laughed again, pushing her knees against his chest. He grabbed at her calves, feeling a sudden, momentary lunge of passion within him. He won-

47

dered at himself. Only a few hours earlier, he had thought he could never again feel casual desire for a woman. And now, he had already made love to one woman on the beach and was looking up at this knowing sprite with the same kind of impulse.

"You've got a dirty mind," she said, as if she could read his thoughts.

"My name is Kevin," he replied, "and my mind is far from dirty."

"All right, Kevin, old buddy, how about letting go of my legs? They bruise easily, especially the way you're hanging on to them."

"They're beautiful."

"I know they are."

He released his hold and swam a few yards from the edge, keeping his gaze on her. She rose to a standing position, a calculated movement, her eyes half-closed, her hips thrust ever so slightly forward.

"You like?" she asked.

"Very much," he answered, paddling close to the edge, craning his head backward for a better look.

"You'll do."

"Thanks a lot."

"My name is Sheri. I thought I might play some tennis this afternoon—providing, of course, that I find someone to play with."

"It just so happens that I'm a tennis nut."

"Maybe you're a nut, period."

He made a quick grab for one of her ankles, meaning to pull her into the pool. But she quickly stepped away from his grasp.

"Until later," she said.

"What time?"

"Around one-thirty."

"I'll be there," he said.

"I bet you will, at that," she said confidently.

She gave him the benefit of a swish of hips as she

48

turned to walk away. The swimsuit fitted her buttocks like a second skin. Kevin became aware of someone beside him in the water. Turning, he saw the teenager who had been testing the diving board.

The boy was grinning broadly. "Hey," he said, "how'd you like to get your hands on those, huh?"

"She's too old for you, kid."

"Man, nothing's too old for me."

The kid pulled himself up on the edge of the pool, resting on his forearms, hungrily watching Sheri's retreat. Kevin shoved away, swimming toward the other end of the pool. He let his arms rise and fall slowly, wanting more of that good fatigue in his muscles.

Sheri slammed the door behind her, angry with herself, angry that she had allowed herself the luxury of fooling around with Kevin at the swimming pool. What was wrong with her? Didn't she have enough to think about without flirting with every dumb tourist who happened along?

She looked around the room, not really seeing it, because it was too much like so many other rooms in her past and she had stopped being able to tell them apart. It seemed almost as if she had spent the greater part of her life in just one room like a prisoner. She slumped into a chair, legs stretched out before her, her hands resting on her bare midriff. Not that it mattered, but if she really concentrated could she possibly remember the number of rooms like this one she had slept in?

And how many men?

How many damned men had there been?

She balled her hands into fists and pounded her stomach senselessly, fighting her own anger, wondering what in hell was happening to her. She suddenly leaped to her feet and ripped her swimsuit off. Naked and strangely cold, she half-ran across the width of the room and leaped into the still unmade bed. She crawled between the sheets and pulled them over her head, burying her face in the soft luxury of the pillow.

The linen smelled like him, she thought. She could still smell him beside her, his manhood alive and pulsating, his eyes with that funny glaze. She wanted to forget him and all the others, the countless others—

She rolled to her side and huddled herself into a small ball, unconsciously assuming the fetal position. She tried to blot everything from her mind and failed.

What was wrong with her? What in hell was eating at her? She had been perfectly all right a few moments ago. Then something had seemed to take hold of her and now she was sick of herself, sick of what she had become.

There was no one whom she could blame, a knowledge that always rankled. Her parents had been good, substantial people who had tried to give her the proper kind of upbringing. Home had been a white frame house with green shutters in a small Midwestern town—home had been laughter and good times and the odor of good cooking permeating the house. Home had been two older sisters who never caused any trouble.

But Sheri had caused trouble from the start. Why? What was within her, deep inside, that had caused her to be different? She had known she was not like her sisters by the time she was thirteen and still in junior high. She had let the boy next door—sixteen and the star halfback on the football team—take her in his bathroom. His parents had come home unexpectedly and found what was going on.

Sheri's mother and sisters had changed toward her after that, as though she had caught some horrible disease which they were afraid of catching. Hell with them, she had thought, and gone her own way. At fifteen, she had stayed the night with three boys in a motel. Her father had tried to claim rape, but he could not make it stick, because of Sheri's reputation around town. Soon after she had run away from home, fed up with the happy people all around her. There had been a few months with a carnival, stripping in front of faceless men. She had been amused when she could make them desire her. For the first time she realized her power over men. Until then she had only received a physical gratification out of giving herself. When she learned that she could control men with her body, she drifted away from the carnival and looked for greener pastures in Chicago.

There she met Frankie. His last name, as it turned out, had never mattered—he had used several. Frankie had been young and handsome, with money enough to do as he wished. He had taken her to Florida, spending as if money grew on trees, and she never had asked where it came from. She had found out the hard way.

Frankie had been shot down and killed outside a supermarket he had tried to rob while she waited for him in the car, thinking he had gone inside for some cigarettes.

The cops had not believed Sheri's story. She had spent three days and two nights in jail, listening to the inevitable questions, giving the same answers over and over. Finally she had managed to be alone with the fat, middle-aged detective long enough to seduce him, and that had been that.

From Florida, she had gone to New Orleans, Memphis, St. Louis and Chicago again, a never-ending circle of greedy men and tainted money.

She had gone home only once. H~~ family had been surprisingly, painfully, courteous to her, but conversation had been impossible. They could not make small talk, naturally. Nor could she shriek at them, tell them all to go to hell as she wanted to do. She was merely a guest—and a very comfortable one.

Again she had fled the familiar surroundings, never to return, not even for her mother's funeral. In the interim, there had been men, and more men. She could not remember them all—she could remember very few of them. Once in Cleveland she had met a real nut who had wanted her to make love to other men while he watched. The money had been good, so she had gone along with him, but the memory of those months was a nightmare.

And then there had been Sammy.

Good old Sammy.

The most wonderful stinker in the world.

They couldn't make two like Sammy, not in one generation.

She had met him in a small, dim bar off Broadway in New York, where he played the piano at night for pennies. He was full of words and ideas and he had made her laugh for the first time in months, so she had gone to his apartment.

He had had big ideas on how to get money. Before long she and Sammy were a twosome, traveling the circuit. She did as he told her and the money was good and the life not bad, if you forgot all the old fat men out for one last fling, grunting and groaning as if they might die in a moment.

And now?

And now she was alone again, without Sammy's arm to guide her. Suddenly she was frightened. Was she fully capable of making out on her own? She had been so careful to choose the right man, the one she thought she could part from some money, and yet she had just caught herself flirting with someone else. Sammy would not have allowed as foolish a slip as that.

She rolled around in the warm sheets, remembering the force and strength in Jim. Love with him had been exciting, the way it had been in her girlhood before she lost count of her men.

She was only twenty-two, but already half-dead within. There had to be more to life than she had experienced.

Was it too late to change her mind? She wanted the birthright she had junked, the comfort and respectability of holding her head high as she walked down any street.

A man like Jim could give her that. But he was married—all the good ones were married.

His wife was a cold fish, Jim had told her, a woman who could not give him the satisfaction he desired.

But Sheri could satisfy him.

The thought warmed her. If she could only get Jim away from that wife of his, the rest would be easy.

She knew how to handle a man like Jim.

She hoped he would be the last. She sometimes felt tired of handling men.

What she hoped for, she guessed, was that someone would worry some day about handling Sheri. About catering to her moods and needs and desires—and who else but a husband could be counted on for that?

She wondered if Sammy had not, in his way, handled and managed her. Maybe that was why she found herself thinking of him when she expected it least.

Wouldn't it be funny if, after she got married, Sammy were to come around and give her life a fillip?

She would have to watch herself, not get all mixed up again if she ever got straightened out.

You sometimes made a mistake, thinking you knew who was on your side and who wasn't.

As a little girl, she had liked boys' sports, had nagged and punched and bragged of her prowess to get on neighborhood baseball teams. A playmate named George—he might have been nine—had been the object of her special envy because he was good at everything.

Except for George, she might have been top dog on the block.

One day she was up at bat and George was catching for the opposing team. Partly by accident, she threw her bat after hitting the pitch—partly by accident, the bat hit George in the head and he had to go to the hospital for a month.

In his absence, instead of becoming top dog, she was barred from all games. It was George, she learned, who had cast the deciding vote among the boys, when they considered letting her on the team.

7

AFTER CHANGING into shirt and slacks, Kevin returned to the snack shop for more coffee.

Smoking a lazy cigarette over his second cup, he found that there was pleasure again in merely being alive, in listening to the sounds of strangers' voices, in looking through a window at sunlight on a lawn.

A time like this was what he had desperately needed.

The waitress came by his table to drop his check. She looked at him expectantly, as though she thought he would speak to her. He smiled, not knowing what to say. She moved away, her tight little buttocks in the green uniform bringing back a memory of Sheri at the swimming pool.

What had gotten into him? He was suddenly like a sailor at the first port in a year.

He wondered whether his ex-wife had left him somehow warped. For months he had tried to satisfy her weird, insatiable desires until he had sickened of demands that had wrung his flesh dry and left him weak and nervous. Sometimes he had wondered how he could manage the strength to rise and face the everyday morning world.

Perhaps he had tried too hard.

He thought of Lili, the poetry of her naked body in the cold moonlight of the beach, the wonder of

55

their lovemaking. He thought of Sheri's cute little buttocks and puffed-out, passionate-looking lips and of her candid questioning eyes.

Just now, watching the waitress walk away, he had had to restrain a startling impulse to reach out and touch her.

Had he gotten as bad as Felice? What did they call a man who could never get enough?

He looked through the window again. Lili was walking toward the coffee shop. Their glances met as she approached the entrance. Without changing expression she turned abruptly and started in the opposite direction.

Kevin quickly paid his bill. He ran out of the coffee shop, was in time to see Lili disappear beyond the hedges that flanked the path. He knew he was playing with fire yet he could not help himself. Something about Lili was forcing him to follow her.

She had paused a few feet from the turn in the path and was looking back the way she had come. A shadow marred the curiously strict beauty of her face. His heart sank for some reason he could not fathom.

She started to walk on. He called her name.

She took two more hurried steps and then stopped, her shoulders showing defeat.

He caught up with her, made her turn to face him, his hands holding her elbows. "What's wrong?" he asked. "You act as if—well, as if you don't want to see me."

"I don't," she replied.

He released her elbows and stepped back, wondering how she could have been so warm and loving last night.

"This is an act," he stated. "You don't really want to run from me. Last night I—"

"Last night never happened," she said quickly and harshly.

"You're not a one-night woman."

"What do you know about me?" Her mouth was down at the corners and she kept glancing around, as if she were afraid. He had almost forgotten for a moment that she was a married woman, that last night had been wrong. "I'm a stranger to you," she went on, "and that's as it should be. Can't you understand that I don't want to see you, that I don't even want to think about you any more?"

"I'm sorry," he heard himself say. "I guess I took too much for granted. I imagined that you might feel as I do." He could barely believe that the words were his. Would he never learn? "I won't bother you after this unless you bother me first. Okay?"

"I won't bother you," she assured him. Briefly, her frown deepened to anguish and then she shook her head and walked away.

"Lili," he called.

She hesitated, not turning.

"The world can be a pretty bitched up place, can't it?" he asked.

"It's what we make it," she said, still not turning. She went her way.

He was sick in his own way, he mocked himself, perhaps sicker than Felice. Lili's attitude was the only sane one under the circumstances—last night was better forgotten.

He had batted his head against a wall for years without success—now he seemed ready and willing to start all over again. He was a romanticist, a fool— he was idealizing a meaningless sexual encounter into a big deal.

If there were such a thing as a meaningless sexual encounter—perhaps there was always a meaning, whether good or evil.

Lili fought panic. She wanted to break into a run, get away from Kevin as quickly as she could. But she forced herself to walk at normal pace, shoulders back, head high, trying desperately not to show the shame she felt.

She reached a small green bench that overlooked the tennis courts, sat down and let the morning sun warm her face.

Sheer intensity of emotion had made her weak. She turned to glance back at last. But Kevin would not follow her, any more than he had followed her last night. For that she gave him credit. Yet she knew that she half-wished he would come to her, that he would force the issue between them.

What issue? What was she hiding from herself? Kevin had discovered her during a weak moment, that was all, and he had taken advantage of her weakness—no, she could not honestly claim he had taken advantage. She had been a full partner in their rendezvous on the beach.

She shuddered involuntarily, despite the warmth of the sun. What could she do next? She and Jim were finished. She had lain awake a long time during the night, nursing the bruises he had given her in his anger, thinking of the love she had known for him once so that it hurt her to be apart from him even briefly. But had that really been love? Or had Jim been a symbol to her, someone she could show off to the other girls? She did not enjoy her ruthless self-evaluation, yet out of habit she had to be honest with herself.

She still found it nearly inconceivable that she could have made love to a stranger. She believed in uprightness and what she had done with Kevin was wrong. Why, at the time, had her instincts betrayed her? Why had wrong seemed right and natural, like an awakening to love? She had enjoyed lovemaking with Jim in the beginning, but not in the same way. Pleasing her husband in bed had been an achievement like getting the house clean, giving Lili the satisfaction of a job well done. If in the performance of her duty she happened to reach a certain satisfaction, so much the better. And after she had stopped admiring her husband's character, there had been no satisfaction at all for Lili in sex.　　　　　　　　　　　..

With Kevin she had reached an ultimate fulfillment, a sense of losing control and of being bodily lifted into a whirling vacuum.

How could one compare such things? She knew she wanted more than a man to satisfy her physically, a man who thought of her and not only of himself.

A couple strode out to the tennis courts below. They began lobbing the ball slowly back and forth. The man was tall and razor-thin. A handkerchief was bound across his forehead to protect the eyes from hair and perspiration. The woman was almost thinner than the man. There was strength in the way she bounded around and swung her racquet. They seemed to be merely volleying, not playing a game. Intent on the ball, neither spoke.

Lili watched them in silence. She had an impulse to yell at them, to make them notice her. She wanted them to know how unhappy she was, what a horrible mess she had made of her life. Was it fair for them to concentrate on a silly game, unmindful of a world that was full of heartache? Were they happy? Could one judge by watching a game?

She rose quickly and walked along the pathway toward the ocean, afraid that if she stayed she might actually intrude on the tennis players. She did not want to make even more of a fool of herself.

The ocean was calm and majestic. Sun glinted off the rolling waves. Far out, a freighter stirred toward the horizon.

Last night along that beach somewhere she had given herself to a stranger.

A man was walking a dog near the water's edge. The man stooped to free the dog from its leash and the dog made a half-dozen circles of dutiful joy before returning to heel. Solemnly, flanking each other, man and dog roamed out of sight.

She had been awake when Jim had returned to the cabin during the small hours. She had remained stiffly on her side of the bed, hearing him stumble in the dark and babble alcoholic curses. He had spoken her name as he got into bed, but she had not answered and he had gone right to sleep. She had felt as if she were next to some horrifying intruder rather than with her husband. When she was sure he was asleep, she had dressed and left the cabin to walk along the lonely beach until the sun was up.

She still had had no breakfast. Earlier, heading for a hot cup of coffee, she had been interrupted by the sight of Kevin through the window.

She turned once more and found herself facing another stroller—Sheri.

The two women stood looking at each other for a long silent moment.

She's beautiful, Lili thought. And sexy.

Sheri wore a short terry-cloth jacket that reached just below her hips, sandals and sunglasses.

She said, finally, "Good morning, Mrs. Thompson."

Lili managed a smile. "You're formal."

"Why shouldn't I be?"

"I don't know. When two women share the same man, they might as well use first names."

"Do you want me to deny what you already know?"

"I want nothing from you, Sheri. Do you want my husband for keeps?"

Sheri's mouth showed her surprise at the question. She lifted a hand to her sunglasses, straightening

60

them on her nose. "I hadn't given it much thought before now. But he really isn't so bad, as men go."

"You can have him if you want him," Lili said tautly.

Sheri snapped, "Are you nuts? Aren't you going to put up any kind of fight?"

Lili brushed past Sheri without another word, not trusting herself to speak, no longer wanting breakfast.

She went back to the cabin, determined on a showdown. But she found Jim still asleep. He lay on his back in the middle of the bed, arms flung to either side. He was on top of the blankets, naked. She remembered all the times she had given herself to that great, strong body and a feeling of disgust welled up within her. She found his pants on the floor where he had left them, searched his pockets for the car keys.

She had to run, she had to get far from the sight of his naked body.

When Lili drove a car, part of her was not in turmoil. She had a basic respect for machinery of all kinds.

More respect, she thought bitterly, than Jim seemed to have for the human body. She felt irritated with Sheri for wanting Jim, a perverse and superficial feeling that would have amused her if she had been capable of being amused.

That stupid girl thought she knew Jim.

What a surprise she had in store.

There should have been a sign on Jim, or in his vicinity, the kind of warning sign they put up for the bears in Yellowstone National Park. Do Not Feed The Animals. They Are Not Tame.

At the edge of the road, nature took advantage of every opportunity. Homely stands of grass extended from parent clumps, thrusting in places through the blacktop. Beneath the gritty soil, Lili visualized a conscienceless slum of jostling greedy roots. Life did not have to be beautiful. She should have known of the amorality at the core of things.

She still expected more of human beings than she did of weeds.

She expected more of herself.

From here on, would she go downhill as she had feared? Had she caught Jim's moral contagion? She had been picked up at a bar last night. She had given herself to a stranger. She was not even sure she felt any scalding shame, as she should have done.

Perhaps after this there would be many bars and many strangers.

Why not?

She passed a roadside tavern, slowed down and stopped.

In spite of the early hour, the bar had two customers. One was Lili. The other was a slender suntanned giant in T-shirt and white shorts who seemed barely past twenty. He was drinking beer. Lili studied him curiously.

Jim at twenty, she thought with a pang, must have looked rather like that.

The young stranger met her gaze. He afforded her a boyish smirk of appreciation, which she realized was meant as a compliment to her beauty.

He raised his glass to shoulder level, as though in a toast, then swallowed long and deep.

He asked, when he put the glass down, "Buy you a drink, lady?"

"Yes," she said. She considered what she would want at this hour of day. "Orange juice, please."

He smiled indulgently. "To each his own." He gave her order to the bartender, made small talk. "Staying around here?"

"I think so," she said truthfully. "I'm not sure how far I've driven. I was roaming, I guess."

"Look no further," he told her grandly. "You've reached rainbow's end."

"Meaning you?"

"Meaning me."

Lili sipped her juice. "You're a handsome child, all right," she conceded. "I take it you're an athlete."

He made a face. "You're right and wrong. You're right, I'm an athlete. You're wrong, I'm no child. As plenty of chicks can testify. If you don't mind my bragging."

"I don't mind," she said mildly. "But some day someone will mind strenuously. Some silly idealistic chick will think you're the greatest thing since they finished the Rocky Mountains. She'll throw in her lot with you, as the saying goes. And when she finds out what a phony you are, she'll no doubt crack up. She'll come to a bad end, talking to strangers in bars."

"Gosh, grandma," the boy said, "what big teeth you have."

She ignored the pleasantry. "Why aren't you doing something useful at this hour of day?" she demanded.

"That reminds me," he said. "I need another beer." He gave his order.

"You'll never make it," Lili told him sadly. "You think you'll be young forever, that you'll never show the chasing and the drinking—" she paused, realizing she was not quite in the present, that she was addressing herself to the ghost of a younger Jim rather than to this boy.

"You're a real fun type," the boy said. "This is some new approach, isn't it?"

"I'm only trying to reach you for your own good."

"I'll tell you a way," he said. In a normal tone of voice, he made a suggestion that employed words she was not used to hearing, not even from Jim.

Her first instinct was to slap his face.

She thought better of it. What was the use?

"No," she told the boy. "We could never make contact. We're on different vibrations. Maybe in different centuries. One of us is a ghost. Or maybe we're haunting each other."

He recoiled. "Lady," he said, his voice soft at last with a kind of horror, "you ought to get off that orange juice kick. It's doing things to your brain."

She walked away from him, satisfied on at least one point about herself.

She was not likely to pick up great numbers of men in bars.

She still felt involved with the previous pick-up.

She suddenly felt a frenzied anxiety to make contact with Kevin.

To talk to him. She looked for a phone booth.

8

KEVIN SAT IN HIS CABIN, telephone cradled against his ear. The ringing ceased and a woman's voice said warmly, "Good morning. Stern, Smith, and Morris."

"Hi, Edna. Kevin Morris talking."

Her laugh of recognition came across the wire. He could picture her at the vast desk, typewriter on the little platform beside her, gray hair fluffy and beautiful.

"Why, Kevin, how nice to hear from you. Getting some rest? Where are you?"

"At a motel on the beach. Spent the night here."

"I hope the sun is shining."

"Gloriously."

"Do you want to talk to Mr. Stern? Mr. Smith is in court this morning."

Kevin hesitated. "I only called to make sure you'd know where you could reach me—if anything comes up."

"Right," Edna said. "Give me the address and phone."

After he had stated them, she continued, "The best thing you can do is forget about the office. Get a lot of exercise and sleep."

"I'll do that, Edna. Tell Mr. Stern I called and where I am. If I move on, I'll let you know."

"You have a good time now, Kevin."

"I will, Edna. Plenty of play and sleep."

He hung up and was startled by a feeling of homesickness that came over him. Could he actually miss his office? What kind of nut was he?

Not the office, but its solidity was what he missed, he realized. He was at some kind of crossroads in his life, apparently, and he sensed in himself a desperate need to keep his directions clear.

He took a deep drag on a cigarette, wondering why his life—of all people's—had to be so confused and mixed up. There were others around him—too many to count—who enjoyed confusion or at least tolerated it. Yet their lives were orderly and content, not like his own.

He thought of his senior law partner. Ralph Stern, ten years older than Kevin, had virtually inherited his partnership from his father, had never battled chaos to make a life of his own. Stern was an easygoing man who had been known to lose important papers but never his temper—nor, come to think of it, a case he expected to win. Ralph's wife, a plump busy little woman, was devoted to him. His three daughters treated him with a loving disrespect that was worth a million bucks. Even though surrounded by funny-looking females, Ralph Stern had it made.

What was he doing, Kevin suddenly asked himself —comparing himself to Ralph Stern, hating the guy for being happy?

He slammed his hand against the top of the dresser, angry with himself. Completely gone was his euphoric mood at waking. He was angry at his helplessness against the torment within him.

The afternoon sun was blazingly hot at the tennis courts. Kevin wondered whether Sheri would show up. He swung his rented racket back and forth a few times, feeling the tightness in his shoulder muscles. He had not played tennis in more than a year. His last opponent had been Felice . . .

Damn it, he had to quit thinking about her. She was no longer part of his life, but he was letting her color his thoughts, his decisions—his future.

He looked up again, saw the trim little figure coming toward him along the pathway. Sheri carried a racquet in her left hand. Her tennis shorts were brief enough to be remarkable. Her blouse accentuated the firmness of her breasts.

"I wondered if you would come," he said.

"I said I would," she replied.

"A lot of people say things."

"My, my." She smiled slightly. "We are bitter today, aren't we?"

"I guess so."

She touched his arm in a gesture of compassion. "You looked so lonely at the pool, that I just had to come. No one has a right to be as lonely as that."

"Does it show that much?"

"It certainly does, sweetie."

He grimaced at the last word, wishing she would not use it.

"Sure it isn't too hot for you?" he asked.

"Are you trying to weasel out of our game?"

"Of course not."

"Then let's not stand here any longer."

"Sheri?"

"What?"

"Are you married?"

She laughed. "Do you think I would be with you if I had a husband?"

"I'm not sure."

"Well, put your mind at ease. I'm not married."

She ran to the far side of the court, readied her racquet and yelled, "Fire away."

He sent a ball easily over the net. He was not prepared for the viciousness of her return. The ball skipped under his backhand and he finished swinging at nothing with a wry grin on his face. They volleyed back and forth. He stopped being surprised at her ability. She played an angry, slashing kind of game, attacking the ball as if it were a personal enemy. Perspiration dripped down the middle of his back, across his forehead.

The physical activity felt better and better. He was glad that Sheri was good. Once he got back the feel of the game, he began playing as viciously as she did. Neither of them spoke. There was no sound but the impact of the racquets against the ball, the dull noise the ball made as it skidded across the court.

"How about a set?" he asked her, during a brief pause.

"I'm willing," she replied, grim-lipped.

She made him work for his points. Her forehand was amazingly strong and accurate for so small a person. But gradually his superior power and ability began to pay off. The last two games of the set were routs in his favor. He won the set, 6-2, with no sense of taking unfair advantage. He had worked hard for victory.

She came around the net after the final point, her right hand extended in congratulation. Her grip was firm and strong as he shook her hand.

"You're more than I bargained for," she said between deep breaths.

He laughed. "You're no slouch either."

"I've played a little," she admitted.

They stood in the hot sun, each soaked with perspiration, each breathing thirstily. She ran the back of her hand across her eyes, squinting against the brilliant blue sky.

"You're stronger than you look," he said.

"I have my points."

"They're clearly visible, even from here."

"Are you normally a lecher, or does something special in me bring out the animal in you?"

"You like bringing out the animal and you know it."

"Maybe I do, at that." She was staring at him, as if really seeing him for the first time as an individual. "You aren't such a bad guy, after all. This morning, I got the idea you were just out for a quick good time. Now, I'm not sure."

"Why don't we have a couple of cool drinks and discuss it?"

"I've got to have a shower first."

"And then?"

"And then, sweetie, we'll see. Don't rush me."

"Why not? Maybe I like to rush things."

She laughed, raising a hand to his cheek. She ran her fingers along the line of his jaw and then his lips. He felt the beginning prod of desire within him, once more was surprised by it.

She started to turn, hesitated and frowned. Kevin followed the direction of her gaze and saw the big man coming toward them with a scowl. He recognized Lili's husband and knew there would be trouble.

"You'd better go," he said quickly.

She gave him a startled look. "You know him?"

"Not well."

"Then, why—" She did not finish the question.

Jim came close, his shoulders hunched as though prepared for attack.

"Damn you," he shouted at Kevin. "First my wife, now her."

"Look," Kevin started to say, "there's no sense—"

The blow came before Kevin could defend himself. He saw the swing of the other man's arm, the big hand coming for his face. The blow caught him in the mouth as he tried to duck, spilling him to the ground.

He lay on his back, wiping a hand across his mouth. There was blood on the back of his hand.

Jim stood above him, eyes wild, mouth contorted. Kevin rolled away, a dull anger throbbing in his brain, and rose to his knees.

Sheri shrieked Jim's name as the big man started after Kevin again. Looking more child-like than ever in contrast to Jim, she sprang at him, pulled him half around to face her. "Stop it, Jim. Right now."

Kevin had regained his feet. Sheri kept hanging on to Jim, rather like a bulldog pup.

"Let him go," Kevin told her.

She did not even bother to look in his direction.

Jim swung around, bellowing, "I'm going to smash his face in."

Kevin stepped toward them. In part his anger was already fading at the absurdity of the small woman trying to hold the crazed giant. He laughed aloud.

"My turn," he told Sheri. "Get out of my way and let me spill his blood."

Jim's eyes were half-shut. He balanced on the balls of his feet, suddenly looking as if he might fall on his face. Sheri put her hands against his muscular chest. She probably thought she was holding him back—actually she was holding him up.

"You go to my cabin," she coaxed. "I'll be right there."

"Keep away from my wife," Jim growled at Kevin over Sheri's head. He turned and stamped away.

Kevin patted his mouth. The bleeding had stopped.

Sheri had dropped her sunglasses and now she bent over, picking them up. One of the lenses had been cracked and she poked a finger through it, scattering glass on the ground. She looked at Kevin with a slow uncertain smile.

"Well," she said, "that pretty much rips it, doesn't it?"

70

Kevin scooped up his racquet, not trusting himself to speak. Finally he managed, "You and he—you've been friends."

"I suppose you think I'm a real bitch, don't you?"

Again, he did not answer.

"Well, haven't you been running around with his wife?"

Kevin felt outraged. "That's not your business," he said.

"I'm making it my business."

"Why?"

"You wouldn't understand."

"Try me."

"No. It wouldn't do any good."

"Sheri," he said slowly, trying to formalize his words, trying to picture himself before a jury, pleading a case, "listen to me. That man is violent. He's a case. I don't think you ought to get involved with him. You might get hurt."

"He wouldn't hurt me."

"You sound awfully confident."

"Sweetie," she said, giving him the benefit of a quick, meaningless smile, "there's one thing I know in this world, and that's men. Don't give me any advice about men."

"You're an idiot," Kevin said in exasperation. "And probably also a troublemaker."

She lost control of her temper. "How would you know?" she snapped. "I can look at you and read you like a book. You've had a smug, righteous life all the way till now. You haven't had to fight any devils in yourself. You don't know about me. You can't know. Your kind lives in another world from mine, a world where people are kind and polite because they like it that way. Don't give me any free advice, mister —I'm full up to here with advice from your kind." She gestured at her throat with one hand. "And I know what kind of hypocrite you are. You took one look at me this morning and decided I'd be a nice roll in the hay. Well, let me tell you something—you were right, I'm good. Better than you'll ever have." She ran her hands over her stomach, churning her hips suggestively. "I know what this body's for, and I know how to use it. I can make guys like you pop their damned eyes out whenever I want." She took a deep sigh, shaking her head sadly, as if the very thought of him were enough to make her sick.

"Are you finished?" he asked.

"With you, yes."

"But not with him, is that it?"

"Never with him."

"And it doesn't make any difference to you that he's married?"

"Did it make any difference to you, when you chased after his wife?"

"That was impulse, not part of a plan. Two wrongs don't make a right."

"Get lost," she said.

"You are a little bitch," he marveled.

"Sure I am. I don't deny it. I know what I want and I know how to go after it."

"Okay," he conceded. "You'd better run along. You promised that big bastard you'd meet him in your cabin. You'd better go give him whatever you had in mind."

"I will. And you think about it, sweetie. Think of me between the sheets with him. Think of that, and I'll be laughing at you."

"Beat it," he said, feeling his anger return in a new and terrifying form.

"Sure, sweetie. Sure thing."

She turned and scampered away, lithe and foot-loose as a child of twelve.

He was probably not the only person in the world, Kevin thought, who had needed a vacation.

There might not be many like Sheri but how many did it take? And everyone who came in contact with her would probably feel the need of time off before very long.

She was not like Felice, the sick and lovely and damned.

Sheri was as earthy as dust and grime though infinitely more appealing.

A nice old-fashioned girl—as old-fashioned as the first scarlet woman that men had been warned against by their once-bitten, twice-shy forefathers.

9

DAMN EVERY STINKING one of them, Kevin thought.

He walked toward his cabin, for the first time appreciating the fragmentation of his life. There seemed to be no sanctuary, no line where he could withdraw and orient himself. He had stopped knowing what to expect of himself, what kind of man he was, what company he belonged in.

How could he keep going without knowing where he was headed? He closed the cabin door behind him and leaned against it, feeling the weariness of a losing struggle against overwhelming odds. He had wanted normalcy and serenity. He had imagined that, with a sane approach and some time off for rest, he would forget Felice automatically. The half-sane life he had shared with her would recede, he had hoped, into the past. This trip had been intended as a fresh start in his own soul, a search for what was good and decent in life.

And now?

Within less than twenty-four hours, he had involved himself in a crazier situation than the one with Felice. Lili was a beautiful, love-starved woman, cheating on her husband and, what might be even more ominous, fleeing from any tenderness, any commitment. Sheri was a super-tramp, a girl in whom every other quality had been twisted to serve her sexuality. And Jim—Jim would probably make headlines someday when the savage within took over for keeps.

74

And, of course, there was himself—Kevin Morris.

He moved away from the door, tossing the tennis racquet to a chair. He considered packing his bags and leaving this place, seeking sanctuary somewhere else from the chance evils of life.

The telephone interrupted his thoughts. He looked at the instrument as though it had personality. How often had that block of plastic, unknowing, unfeeling, been the messenger of evil? He was reluctant to answer.

The ringing ceased abruptly and he breathed a sigh of relief.

In the bathroom mirror, he saw that his lower lip was swollen only slightly. From the force of Jim's blow, he had expected to find that his whole mouth was shattered. He smiled grimly and bent to wash his face.

He returned to the other room and stared hard at the telephone, almost wishing that it would ring again. Who could have been calling? His office? One of the three people he had met at this motel? For some reason, he thought of Ralph Stern, his partner, and Ralph's face when he heard, "Your home is on the line."

One thing was sure—the call had not been from home—Kevin had no home. He found himself wondering what Felice was doing, right at this very moment. He could imagine. She would be doing what she did best in the world, what she was most practiced at. The thought did not rankle as it had in the past. He could now imagine her with another man and not feel sick and blind with hurt. Perhaps he was coming out of it. He hoped so. Bitterness and remorse were unpleasant companions.

Yet, part of him would always belong to Felice— the years, the living time that no one could give back.

He remembered the cocktail party where they had

first met. She had been apart from everyone else, as if surrounded by her own special little world, invisible to everyone but Kevin. Alone in a corner of a large crowded room, sipping martinis, making mild conversation, they had somehow recognized that their meeting was important.

He had taken her home. The night had been one of those absurdly romantic San Francisco settings, with the fog rolling across the city and the fog horns from distant ships making the Orient seem near. She had had a small apartment—she had asked him up for a nightcap. They sat on the couch and listened to fog horns and told each other things that neither one had ever told anyone else.

And then she had been in his arms. Her mouth had at first been soft and pliant, only to turn demanding. Before he had paused to wonder what was going to happen, they had been lying naked side by side, exploring and straining. He had not been inexperienced —far from it—and had been wryly astonished when she fought him at the last moment, refusing him final victory.

"No," she had whispered tautly. "No, Kevin. Please."

His emotions had been almost beyond control, but even then there had been a dread in him that she might be lost to him if he crossed her. At first, he had been angry at her for letting him go so far and then refusing him. His anger had ended when she told him she was a virgin.

"I didn't think there were any left," he had said.

"I'm an old-fashioned girl."

That had been the moment he had known that he loved her. He had been a great fool, he thought. They had lain there together, making love without experiencing its ultimacy. She had whispered of other

76

ways for them to satisfy each other. He had known what she meant.

But when he had left her apartment early the next morning, he had felt a trifle dirty.

Yet he had known he would see her again.

A month later, they were married.

The telephone rang once more.

This time, he answered.

"Kevin?" The voice was female.

"Yes?"

"It doesn't sound like you." He recognized Lili's voice. "Are you all right?"

"Of course. Why wouldn't I be?" he asked harshly. "What do you want?"

"When you put it like that, I don't want anything." There was a sound of hurt feelings in her voice. "Forget it."

"Don't hang up," he pleaded.

"Why shouldn't I?"

"Lili, I—well, after the way you treated me earlier today, I didn't think I'd be hearing from you again."

"I'm sorry about that. It couldn't be helped."

"Why not?" he asked.

"It's too long a story."

"I've got plenty of time."

"In the first place," she said slowly, "I'm a married woman."

"But you called me up."

"Yes. It doesn't make sense, does it?"

"Things have to make sense. Sometimes they're hard to understand, though."

There was a long silence between them, broken finally when she said, "I needed someone to talk to."

"And I was handy, is that it?"

"I guess so."

"Where are you?"

"I'm in a bar about ten miles south of the motel."

"Do you want me to join you?"

"I was hoping you would," she said.

Here we go again, he warned himself. He had to be wiser—he had to have profited at least that much—than when he first married Felice. He had just had a run-in with Lili's husband. Was he begging for more?

"Kevin?"

"What?"

"Are you sure you want to come?"

She had guessed his doubts. "I'm sure," he heard himself say. "But I think you should know that your husband just tried to bash my face in."

"Oh, no! Kevin, I'm sorry."

"I'll come, Lili. How do I get there?"

She gave him the directions.

"Wait for me," he ordered and hung up before he could change his mind.

He was tired of questioning himself, tired of looking for reasons in his behavior.

Sheri finished mixing drinks. She turned from the bureau where she kept her ingredients and looked across at Jim. Just how far could she take him? She knew enough about his kind, about the mean and vicious streak that ran below the surface—not too far below. She had seen him earlier in his fury, and could not repress a shudder of anxiety at the recollection.

He returned her look with a black frown. "Do I get that drink or not?" he asked.

She summoned her courage. "When you remember how to be courteous to a lady, then you can have your drink."

He laughed disparagingly. "Who the hell's the lady around here?"

78

"Go jump off a cliff, Mr. Banker-man," she taunted him. "And on your way out of here, don't look back."

He raised his hands in a helpless, small-boy gesture. "Honey," he soothed, "I was only kidding."

"I don't like that kind of kidding."

"Do I have to beg now?"

"You wouldn't be you if you begged, would you?"

"I guess not."

She walked across the room, making sure that his eyes were on the smooth, flowing motion of her hips. She could see the change in his eyes, hear the sudden quickening in his breath. Her certainty returned and she smiled as she handed him his drink.

She took a chair near him, cuddling up with her legs tucked beneath her. "Jim, what's the matter with you?" she asked.

He seemed puzzled. "What do you mean?"

"You acted like a wild man out there with Kevin. You can't go around a place like this beating up people. You're supposed to be an intelligent, civilized man. What would your banker friends think of you if they saw you acting like an ape?"

"To hell with them," he snapped.

"I don't think you mean that."

He did not comment. He was removed from her now, drifting in a world of his own. She did not interfere. More and more he reminded her of Sammy, although Sammy had usually managed to keep his head when things went wrong. A good man in a pinch, calm and serene—yet he could be violent like Jim when the violence served a purpose.

He finished his drink, put the glass on the floor beside him and sat immobile with his hands clenched. She saw the whites of his big knuckles and knew he was going through a tortured moment of anger. Sure, he frightened her. But if she could harness that anger of his she could have him for her own. She caught herself thinking, *if Sammy were only here,* and then realized what she was admitting to herself. She had to do her own thinking now. Sammy, of course, would not have helped her to a permanent relationship with Jim.

"The bitch," Jim suddenly exclaimed.

"I'm sure that hurts her, having you call her a name."

His voice softened. "I don't understand her," he said.

"Never try to understand a woman."

"Why not? That's an old cliché, and you know it," he insisted. "I understand you. I know what you want. You want a man and that's enough for you. But not her, never her." His voice was rising again. "She wants some kind of a saint pussy-footing around the house." He smacked a closed fist into the palm of his hand. "Do you know she went out last night with that bastard and let him have her? Did you know that?"

"Calm down, Jim."

"Don't tell me to calm down, damn it."

She rose and went to the window, afraid to let him see her face. She had not enjoyed his definition of her as wanting a man and nothing more. What did he know?

Jim was a stubborn, egotistical fool, and she would gain nothing by arguing. What he required was handling.

"Why do you put up with her?" she asked, not turning to face him.

There was no answer. She felt her heart skipping a beat. She had either made her point—or else she had gone too far and lost her chance.

She turned slowly.

The look he gave her was one of calculation. "You

80

think I'm a damned fool for not divorcing my wife. Is that it?"

"That's it."

He laughed. "Honey, in my position a person doesn't get a divorce just because he wants one. I handle people's money. They have to trust me. A divorce is always a mark that you've failed in something. I've never failed in my life and I'm not starting now."

She felt as though control were slipping through her fingers. She had thought she understood him—now he had surprised her.

"Suit yourself," she said sullenly.

"Besides," he continued with a disagreeable smirk, "Lili is a part of my existence back home. Everyone there thinks of us as inseparable."

"Bull," she snapped. "The first chance you got, you gypped on her. You took one look at me and came running. You've probably done the same thing before. You aren't kidding anyone, Jim."

"Let's not talk about it."

"Okay."

"Come here," he commanded. "I've got something on my mind."

"What, for instance?"

"Don't be coy with me. It's too late for that."

"I'm hot and sweaty," she said. "I've got to take a shower."

"Right now?"

"Right now."

"I'll help you."

She laughed, excited in spite of herself. He had so much going for him, if only he knew it, if only he realized how much she really wanted him, not just in the physical sense, but in all the other ways too.

"You're a real card, Jim."

"You bet I am."

81

She unbuttoned her blouse, removed her brassiere. His eyes were full of desire. She ran her fingers across her bare breasts, fingering the nipples, pleased with herself.

He rose to his feet, big and commanding. She said quickly, "No—not yet, Jim. I want to watch you at the same time."

He pulled his shirt off. Half a room apart, they slipped out of their clothes. His nakedness aroused her—she wanted to reach out and touch him. She fought her feelings, made herself wait. When he tried to grab her, she stepped away laughing.

"I told you," she said, "I have to take a shower."

She ran for the bathroom. He caught up with her inside the bathroom door and his hands were crushingly strong as he turned her around to face him. She threw her arms around him, moved against him, feeling the shudder of his body against hers. They backed slowly into the shower, their mouths locked together in a frenzy of ecstasy. Under the pelting water she was stirred into further passion. The world began revolving before her eyes and nothing mattered but the sheer pleasure of sharing herself with him.

Later, in the other room, she was conscious of being carried to the bed with casual tenderness.

She whispered in his ear, "Jim, you're the greatest, the most—"

His teeth were nibbling at her wet shoulders. She felt a resurgence of passion, locked her arms around his neck and pulled him down beside her. Their bodies writhed together, straining to a peak of feeling.

In the beautiful, lustful act, she lost for a little while the shame and defeat and sorrow that were otherwise always with her. Some kind of reverse reaction took place that wiped away the years and their ugly stains. She was like a girl of thirteen again, giving a boy her half-formed virginal body.

10

ONE WALL OF the tavern was blue-tinted glass over-looking the beach and ocean. Another wall consisted almost entirely of a huge brick fireplace, and the one opposite contained as many paintings as could possibly be hung on it, each with a small, neatly typed price tag in its corner.

A grumpy-faced bartender in a soiled white jacket was leaning on his elbows, his gaze fixed without friendliness on two young men in jeans and over-sized sweaters, who obviously were interested only in each other.

Lili sat at a table alone watching the waves beat themselves against the unmoving rocks. More than half an hour had passed since she had spoken to Kevin, and he was still not here. Would he come? She was beginning to doubt it.

A girl at another table giggled uncertainly. Lili glanced in her direction, saw that there were two of them, bosomy, somehow dusty, with too much eye make-up. The girls were out for a good time, Lili thought, waiting for someone or something to come and happen to them, to give them romance for this day. How different was she from them? She was also here, was she not?

She closed her eyes and remembered the contours of Kevin's face, wondered what her life would have been if she had met him before meeting Jim.

83

She told herself that her thoughts were too young to fit her.

She had always been romantic. She had waited for the day when a handsome man would sweep her off her feet, give her a home, family and all the other answers. Well, Jim had come along. He was certainly big and handsome and she certainly had imagined that he was the key to her dreams. Could she ever trust her dreams again?

Still no sign of Kevin.

He, too, had failed at marriage—he had told her as much.

The failure of a marriage was personal, a stigma which could never be wiped out. Kevin showed the scars.

She saw him coming in just as she was ready to give him up, his shoulders hunched forward, his eyes searching for her. He was wearing dark-colored slacks and a tan sports shirt out at the waist. He stopped a moment inside the door, as if not sure that he meant to come the rest of the way inside. Then he saw Lili and walked toward her with a smile. The smile, she thought, was tired.

"Hello," she said.

He sat. She could see the red puffiness around his lip and damned Jim for being an idiot.

"You don't have to stay long," she said.

"Let's not question each other, Lili," he said earnestly. "I came because you called me. It just may be that you and I are the same kinds of fool. Let's just accept the fact that we are what we are and we can't do much about it."

"You make us sound so trapped."

"Aren't we?"

"Maybe."

He gestured to the bartender, who came slowly and heavily toward their table. Kevin ordered drinks and offered her a cigarette, which she refused. He took his time lighting one for himself.

"I want to clear the air about something," she said.

"What's that?"

"Last night."

He looked at her warily. "You told me this morning that it never happened."

"I know what I told you." She paused, searching for the right words. "Kevin, I'm not sure how I ought to put this. I've never been in a similar situation before, believe it or not. I don't know what came over me—no, that's not right. I do know, but it's a personal matter that doesn't concern you. I think I've involved you in my troubles and I'm sorry. I'd advise you to get clear of me—well, maybe after today."

"Don't worry about me," he said.

She glanced down at the waves. "I thought I would feel ashamed when I talked about it. I don't."

"Why should you be ashamed?" he asked. "We shared a beautiful moment, one that I'll never forget, no matter how hard I might try."

"You're a very sweet person, Kevin."

He made a wry face. "I'm not sure I like to be called that."

The bartender brought their drinks. Lili marveled at how easy and comfortable she felt with this man of whom she knew almost nothing. She knew she was a person of more than usual reserve who made few close friends. She had not even made a friend of the man she had married. But Kevin seemed like someone she might have known for years.

She touched his puffed lip with her fingertip. "I'm terribly sorry about Jim. He sometimes—"

"Forget it," he interrupted. "I suppose I had it coming. A man has a right to be angry under the circumstances." He grinned. "Besides, I think he was angrier about—" He shook his head, not finishing the sentence.

"About what?" When he did not speak, she insisted, "Tell me, Kevin."

"There's nothing to tell."

"I think you're keeping something from me. Please don't. Let me feel I know at least one person who's spontaneous and sincere."

"I was playing tennis with a girl named Sheri."

"I know her."

"Your husband came along. It wasn't even a fight. He said something about you and me and then hit me in the face. I didn't do one damned thing about it."

"I suppose, to a man, that's important." She could picture him, lying there, Jim towering over him, Sheri in the background. She knew she might as well change the subject.

"Kevin, I wanted to see you again for another reason too. I want to apologize for the way I acted this morning. I was horrible, and I have no excuse. Also, I—" she hesitated, not sure of how to put it— "I wanted your advice. You told me you were divorced. I'm going to divorce Jim. There's nothing left for him and me. This trip was supposed to solve our problems, but we seem only to have acquired more problems."

"If you're really set on divorce," he said slowly, "the first thing would be to see a lawyer. I happen to be one—but I don't handle divorce cases. They're not my line."

She felt a curious physical revulsion at the mechanics of divorce. But it was more revolting, she reminded herself, to get punched and sworn at.

"Of course," she explained, "I've given thought to what I'm doing."

"It isn't an easy thing to go through emotionally," Kevin said. "Believe me, I know from experience."

"I don't like to think about it, but it has to be done."

"It's a long and involved process. Of course, if you have the money, you can always skip over to Nevada and take up residence there for six weeks."

They needed a change, she and Jim had assured each other, before they started on this trip.

There would be changes, all right.

"I think we both need a little cheering up," Kevin said. "How about driving into Los Angeles and having dinner with me?"

"I couldn't."

"Why not?"

"It wouldn't be right. You know that."

He laughed. He seemed happier than when he had first come in.

"Do you always try to do right, Lili?" he asked her.

"I suppose so."

"Has it always worked?"

She exclaimed, "How could it? All I do is try. If I go to L. A. with you, Kevin, promise me one thing?"

"I won't promise anything. Not the way I feel."

She laughed wistfully. "That's a young thing to say. And how do you feel?"

"Lili, you're beautiful. I sit here and look at you, remembering you last night, and I'd be lying if I promised not to let it happen again."

She gasped.

He leaned across the table, taking her hands in his. "I don't give a damn whether you're married or not, whether you're going to get a divorce or not. I know only that I want to spend this evening with you and whatever comes, let it come. Shall we leave now?"

She rose, no longer convinced that she wanted to do what was right.

11

SHERI STIRRED DROWSILY. She could hear the uneven breathing of the big man beside her before she opened her eyes. She rolled on to her side and looked at him. The thought crossed her mind that this was his moment of helplessness. If you wanted to get ahead of Jim, the time would be while he slept.

She rested her head against his naked chest and ran her hand across his stomach. He had no reaction—his sleep was deep. She touched the tight muscles along his thigh and was thrilled by them. He was all man.

He was for her.

And to hell with everything else.

After a while he opened his eyes and murmured, "Lili?"

"No," she laughed. "I'm Sheri."

He sighed. "Good. Great."

"Go back to sleep. I want to lie here and look at you."

"Don't you ever get enough?"

"I've had enough now," she said.

"You're lying."

"I know."

"I've had it, Sheri."

"I know that, too."

"Give me some time, just a little time."

"I'll give you all the time in the world. We make such sweet music together. I never want to leave this bed. I want to be here with you for the rest of my life."

"You're the most beautiful whore in the world," he said. "And the most talented."

"Tell me you'll never leave me, Jim. Say it."

He was silent.

"Please, Jim, give me hope." She realized that she was begging and did not give a damn. She never had had to beg before, but this was an appropriate time. Jim could be her last chance before she came to disaster and she had to make the most of her hours with him, no matter at what cost.

He put his hand roughly against her shoulder and pushed her away from him. He held her at a distance of some inches while he searched her face as though for a clue to something within her that would allow him to answer her correctly.

"What do you want from me, Sheri?" he finally asked.

"You know. Deep down, you know."

"Is that all you can say?" he snapped, his eyes narrowing.

She cradled her head against his shoulder, as if to force into him the knowledge of how much she cared. She had not bargained for this reaction in herself and she was frightened by it. She could not say the words she wanted to say and that Jim wanted to hear. Three words—I love you. She had said them when she was lying but now they were true and could not be uttered. Why had this happened to her? After all the years, all the countless men, to fall for one and to find yourself too bashful to tell him—

"Forget it," she heard herself say.

"You don't mean that."

"No."

"You know what kind of guy I am, Sheri," he said slowly. "You knew from the beginning. I'm out for a good time. I have a lousy wife and I have to search around. You're not the first and I don't think you'll be the last." He smiled a funny kind of smile that did not touch his eyes. "You're the best, I'll give you that. I'd hate to tell you how many women have talked to me in bed just as you're doing now, but you top them all. Not one of them could hold a candle to you."

"But I'm just an easy tramp, is that it?"

"Tell me what you want. Put it in words."

"I want you. It's that simple."

"And that complex."

"A divorce wouldn't kill you."

"We're back to that," he said disgustedly.

"We're back to that."

"How do I know about you? What do I know about you. You've got a cute little body and you sure as hell know how to use it, but that isn't enough, not for a guy like me. I live in a different world from yours, honey, a world that you wouldn't understand. There's nothing we can do about it."

"Why not?" she insisted.

"Don't nag me."

She felt helpless. He seemed to have closed his mind, leaving her two choices—take it or leave it. She was confused. Before this, it had always been the man who had done the begging in his relationship with her. Now the situation was reversed. Had she lost some of her talent? She was hard and smart, never sucker enough to be trapped by her own emotions. She had better remember her standards for herself—and live up to them.

He said, "I feel like I haven't got a backbone left. All that work." He laughed.

She rolled away from him, sudden anxiety tearing at her insides. She was in no mood for exercising her special brand of charm. What did he think she was—a machine with no feelings?

"What's the matter now?" he asked.

"Nothing."

"Are you hungry?"

"No."

"You sure? Let's call the dining room and have them send some food."

"I don't want anything to eat."

"Are you mad at me?"

"You might say that."

"You came into this with your eyes wide open, Sheri," he said gruffly. "Don't make it hard for yourself."

Earlier she had been unable to tell him she loved him. Now she was too choked with fear and disappointment to utter a single sound about anything.

"Honey," he continued in a softer voice, "I can't divorce her. Maybe you can't understand that, but it's a simple fact of my life. I've got plans. A divorce would ruin those plans."

She still could not answer him.

He rolled against her back, his hard thighs pressing her buttocks. With one hand he began gently to caress her breasts. She could feel desire building within her body as though at the flick of a switch. Horrified with herself, she fought against giving in to him, not wanting him to know her full weakness for him.

I'm a package of flesh to him, she thought. Nothing more.

He wheedled, "Don't be mad at me."

She remained silent.

He twisted her breast angrily, cruelly. She screamed in startled anguish.

"That's better," he said. "I thought you might be dead."

"You'll be dead if you try to make love again today."

"That's a quaint way of putting it."

"I think you'd better go, Jim. I'm tired."

She felt his teeth nibbling her ear. His hands roamed her body, found her urgent and fed the fire within her. Against her will, she felt her hips moving in rhythm with his hands. She pulled away from him, rolled back against him. The depth of his desire touched her and she knew she was lost. She hid her mouth against his. He pulled her closer and triumphantly took her over.

She knew how to handle men.

But she had met a man who knew how to handle women.

She reached an ecstasy that seemed compensation enough for her defeat.

Kevin was content. Pleasant music came from the car radio. Lili was beside him, her head resting against the back of the car seat, her eyes half-closed. He could make her happy, he thought, while they were together. The feeling was wonderful.

He turned away from the coastal highway and toward Los Angeles. Eventually the road led into Hollywood. Kevin had never cared too much for Los Angeles. As a San Franciscan, he found the garishness and heat of the more southerly city almost more than he wanted to bear. But this evening he had an entirely different reaction.

Lili said, "I'm not exactly dressed for any place fancy."

He smiled. To Kevin, she looked wonderful in her simple skirt and sweater and low-heeled shoes.

"Cheeseburgers and beer would go great," she said.

"That wasn't exactly what I had in mind."

She laughed happily. "You don't have to impress me, Kevin. You've already impressed me."

"Maybe we can find a small, intimate place with a checkered tablecloth and candlelight and wine."

"You're a Romantic."

"Perhaps."

A red light stopped traffic. He used the time to look at the girl beside him. She had a supple, unconscious readiness, sensuous and willing, that surprised him. It was all he could do to keep his hands to himself. The line of her thighs was beautiful against the skirt, the swell of her breasts beneath the sweater was great art. She turned her head and smiled. A horn complained behind him. The light had turned green and he was holding up traffic.

"Once," he said, turning his attention to driving once again, "there was a man who claimed that nothing was ever created more beautiful than woman. I'm tempted to agree."

"Just tempted?" she teased. She added, more seriously, "I know the lines you mean. A woman is a dish for the gods, if the devil dress her not."

Evening traffic grew heavier the closer they came to the city's heart. The rambling homes and bright green lawns of the suburbs were behind them now.

Kevin remembered driving along this very street with Felice. For the first time, his instinctive reaction to the memory of Felice was irritation rather than anguish. What a hell of a lot of devotion he had squandered—

The place he had in mind might still be on a side street in the middle of Hollywood. He drove in circles for some time before he found the street, whose very name he had not recalled. He parked and they walked the half block to the restaurant.

The place was small and dimly lighted, full of

93

atmosphere which would have been phony except for one important saving grace—the food and service had been superb. The walls were natural plaster. There was a tiny circular bar.

"Very nice," Lili whispered as they entered. "And also—" there was laughter in her voice—"quite romantic."

"The food is good," he said.

"You've been here before?" Her look was oddly perceptive.

"Once."

"With your wife." She was not asking a question.

"That's right." He felt an inexplicable concern, which he tried to put out of his mind.

A stiff, sad-faced waiter led them to a table on the far side of the room. The hour was still early for dinner and they started with the place to themselves. Kevin ordered two martinis, and they took their time browsing over king-sized menus. When the waiter brought their drinks, Kevin told him that they would order dinner shortly but not at once.

They touched glasses silently. Lili took a light sip and placed her drink on the table.

She asked, "I've spoiled your good mood, haven't I?"

"Of course not," he said.

"Kevin, I'm going to ask you a personal question. If you want to tell me to mind my own business, I'll understand. But I'm going to ask anyway. Why are you divorced?"

He made himself meet her level gaze.

"I don't know how to answer," he replied.

"Try."

"Is it important to you?"

"It might be." She took another sip from her glass. "I'm failing right now at marriage myself. Maybe

I'd like to know more about the kind of person who fails."

The sense of concern came back to him, stronger than before. He felt suddenly that he had a great deal to say, not about his own marriage, but about Lili's—and not too much time for talking.

"Listen," he urged. "I may have trouble putting this across. I know it's supposed to be wholesome to blame yourself these days, rather than the other fellow. They tell us that being grown-up means a willingness to face the music. That's only true to a point."

He took a deep breath, waiting for a comment, but she made none and he had to go on. "Some people should never marry—they haven't the equipment for it. And if you happen to fall in love with, and marry, one of those people, the marriage will probably fail through no one's fault at all. My wife was a sick woman. As for Jim—" he paused.

He knew why he was concerned.

"What about Jim?"

"I'm frightened for you," he said. "I'm afraid to take you back to him. I wish we could keep on going after we leave this place—maybe down to Mexico. Or else I wish I could take you back to San Francisco with me."

Her eyes turned sad. "If I weren't married," she said, "I'd guess you were proposing."

"If you weren't married," he said, "there would be less urgency to it. That's a rough guy you've got."

She looked so troubled that he had to add hastily, "Don't let me frighten you. Let's say I'm jealous of him."

"Why on earth would you be jealous of Jim?"

"Because you're lovely. Because I want to take care of you and make you smile, not just tonight, but all the nights."

"How can you say that, Kevin?" Her voice was soft with pain. "You don't really know me."

"I know you well," he insisted. "I've known you all my life. We never happened to meet till now, but that was accidental."

Her eyes were a window to another world, the private world they had shared of sea and sand . . .

"Kevin?" she said questioningly.

"Yes, honey?"

"I could fall in love with you," she said, "with no effort at all."

The waiter was hovering nearby, probably listening in on their conversation. Kevin was glad. He wished the whole world had overheard her words.

He motioned to the waiter and, in a carefully controlled voice, ordered dinner.

12

JIM THOMPSON SIGHED deeply and leaned against the jamb of the bathroom door. His rib cage ached with fatigue and there was a nagging, constant pain in the back of his legs. Three times, he thought. Three times in a couple of hours, and he was worn out. He was not as young as he once had been, it seemed. This was the downhill side. There would not be many more days like today.

Throughout his adult life his greatest pleasure had been to make love to women. He had started early and kept up a grueling pace, in which he took much pride. Everything else in his life had been secondary. Sex was primary. Now, perhaps, he had met his match.

He turned his head to glance back at the bed. Sheri lay on her side, her legs bent at the knees. Her small breasts sagged slightly, the roseate nipples soft, and the whole of her sleek femininity looked somehow distorted and out of shape.

He turned on the cold water faucet in the bathroom sink and put his mouth to it. He absorbed the water like an animal that had been deprived.

He switched on the bathroom light and took another look in the mirror. There were new shadows and a beginning fleshiness about his once-rugged face. He could read the signs of dissipation.

A man got old too quickly, he told himself, and then there was nothing left. He was going to be a fat old shell one of these days and the day was approaching much too quickly. What could he do to protect himself? He was Jim Thompson, eternally young, eternally on the search for a new woman—no one expected anything else from him. A thrill hunter, he thought, and laughed harshly. He repeated the phrase in his mind, looking at the mirror and wishing suddenly that he was someone else.

But he was Jim Thompson.

As a boy he had been brutal without knowing it, using his fists against his classmates, setting up the patterns for their conquered little souls, so that they gave him whatever he demanded. A few adults had rebelled against him—a scoutmaster, two or three teachers—and he had used his mother against them. His mother had always been willing to take up his banner whenever he got beyond his own depth. Little Jimmy could never be wrong—it was always the other person's fault.

He had hated his mother and yet in the very hating he had known how to use her, how to let her pamper and take pride in him. Damn her, he thought. His mother was the reason for his being what he was. Why hadn't she had more sense?

In high school, his dexterity and size had given him the edge in any sport. There had been the fools, even then, who had looked up to him as some kind of adolescent deity, who gladly had done his bidding. The thing with the girls had started then. He had found it so easy to get them. He had let them clamor around him, eager merely to touch him. He would pick one out from time to time with whom to share the greatest thing in the world—for a short time.

There had been only one who got the upper hand. He had had her only once and after that she would never have anything more to do with him. He had pleaded with her, almost to the point of getting down

98

on his knees, and still she had refused him. After all these years, her refusal still rankled.

Her name had been Miss James, and he had never called her anything else. She had been his English composition teacher during his junior year, a tall, soft-skinned woman with reddish hair like a halo around a freckled face. Her fingernails had been long and pointedly sharp, always crimson to match her lipstick.

She had asked him to see her after school about correcting mistakes on a theme. He had pleaded the priority of football practice and she had replied in that calm sarcastic manner of hers that unless he came to her room at three, he would be through with football.

The afternoon had been windy, with rain beating the windows. Miss James had been at her desk in front of the classroom, facing a pile of neatly stacked papers. She had always been neat and she demanded neatness of her pupils.

She had looked up and seen him. Her first words had scared him silly. She had handed him a key and said, "Go lock the door. Then come back to my desk and see that you're quick about it."

Dumbfounded, he had done as he was told. She had risen and stood beside him, "You've got quite a reputation around school. Do you deserve it?"

"That depends what you mean."

"Are you as good as they say you are?"

"At what?" There had been a growing nervousness within him, a feeling that she meant to discipline him for something. He had watched her for a long time from a safe distance, liking her looks. Had he been fool enough to shoot off his face?

"You know what I'm talking about, Jim."

"Miss James—" his tone had been defiantly sarcastic— "I'm just an innocent little boy."

She had laughed. The sound had not seemed to fit her. "We'll see," she had said, and, before he had realized it, she had removed her skirt and was lying on the floor, her arms imperiously beckoning him.

"Miss James," he had protested, glancing anxiously at the door and windows.

"Shut up and move," she had commanded.

He had not been able to resist. He had thrown caution to the winds and, the next thing he knew, she was writhing against him, her long fingernails scraping his back.

She had been like nothing he had ever experienced before. Each movement of her hips had pulled him along until that final, bursting moment. Then she had wriggled away from him and rolled him on to his back and done things that made him want her again—

She had given him thrill on thrill until he had thought he would die of excess sensation. But he had liked everything he had felt.

The episode had lasted no more than thirty minutes. In the end, when she had risen and stepped into her skirt again, he had realized that she had not removed her blouse. He had asked her about that.

"That's only for the good ones," she had answered.

"Wasn't I good?"

"You'll do for a boy," she had said and laughed.

Now, twenty years later, he remembered how he had panted after her for months. She had never again let him close to her. Three times, he thought, three times in half an hour and still he had wanted more. Today, three times in a couple of hours and he felt ready for the old soldiers' home.

"It's a lousy ratrace," he said aloud.

Sheri remained as he had left her, contentedly asleep, dreaming her own dreams. He wondered if he figured in them. Probably he did. He was intelligent enough to know Sheri for what she was. Yet that very intelligence was working against him, whispering to him that his search was over, that in Sheri he had found the ultimate female. He could take her home with him and forget about all the rest—the little teenagers with their shining faces and their desiring, inexperienced bodies—the young matrons whose husbands did not understand them—the career girls out for a fling. All of them, every last one of them, could be forgotten.

He slumped into a chair and watched the darkness creep up and envelop the world. The ache grew worse in his loins. He looked again at the bed and now her form was only a dim outline. He could not make out the features of her face and, for a fleeting second, his memory played tricks with him and he was not sure who she was. There had been so damned many.

He wondered where Lili was. She had threatened to divorce him. Let her try. Silent rage seethed through him at the thought of her treachery last night. He remembered striking her, knocking her down, telling her what he would do if she cheated on him again.

She would never divorce him. No woman in her right mind would leave Jim Thompson, no woman ever had, except that damned English teacher and he had been only a boy then.

He stumbled through the dark room, searching for a cigarette. His anger grew when he found none. Suddenly a smoke seemed the most important thing in the world. His lungs ached for the feel of nicotine.

Out of desperation he switched on the light, though he had not wanted to wake Sheri, with her terrible zest for love. He saw a pack of cigarettes on the floor near the bed. Sheri stirred in her sleep.

He picked up the cigarettes and turned off the light.

The cigarette calmed him. His mind went back to Lili. Maybe he would be better off without her, after all. He could explain, one way or another, to the powers-that-be at the bank, might even get a little sympathy from them, if his story was good enough.

"What're you doing?"

Sheri's voice startled him. He stood quite still in the dark, not wanting to talk before he thought things out.

"Jim?" She waited and tried again. "Jim, what in hell are you doing there?"

He sighed. He could not pretend to ignore her. "I'm having a smoke."

"Come here."

"No more, Sheri. Absolutely."

She laughed. "I have my limits, too."

"I was wondering about that."

"Come on, lie down beside me. All I want to do is cuddle up against you."

He remained silent. There was something ghostly about talking to her in the dark, unable to see her. He took another drag on the cigarette, his thoughts drifting back to Lili—and to others.

"Jim, we're meant for each other."

Her voice brought him back in time and place. He grimaced inwardly at the trite phrase she had used. Nevertheless, he found he agreed with her. They were two similar animals, gulping at each other, not shocked by each other. Maybe it could work.

He could hear the sound of her breathing. In the light, she would look fragile—in the dark, that small body was a ferocious bundle of strength that still surprised him. He sat on the edge of the bed. Her hand brushed his back, not in desire, merely to convey that she liked having him near. He had almost used the word love, but he had never believed in love. A woman was meant to be used, and that was that.

102

Love was a myth.

"What're you thinking about?"

"Nothing," he answered.

"Tell me."

"No."

"I want to know."

He resented her intrusion into his thoughts. She should have understood the turmoil he was enduring. Was that too much to ask? But he knew women—they would never give you a moment's privacy, always grilling, wanting to know your thoughts and plans. His mother had been like that, demanding outrageous entry into his very soul.

He felt Sheri moving. Suddenly, her arms were wrapped around his middle. The softness of her cheek was against his back. She said nothing, she merely held him, as if trying to tell him something. He searched his mind for some definition of love that he could believe.

He said, "Maybe it could work out."

"What?" There was unhidden hope in her voice.

"Us."

"Do you mean it, Jim? Really?"

"Why not? Why shouldn't I mean it?"

"Darling," she whispered. She kissed his back.

"Yeah," he said. He ran his hands along his thigh muscles, grateful for their hardness. His legs were still good. He would last a long time yet, a damned long time.

He had found his definition for love.

He laughed and said, "Yeah," again.

13

LILI HAD LOST TRACK of the time. She knew only that she was happy. To all intents and purposes, someone had suddenly walked into her life and put things right for her. She knew that all good things were earned, even happiness—and perhaps she was paying for the evening with the stern guilt sense she wore, like a hair shirt under rather than over the skin.

Kevin sipped his brandy and smiled.

"I like to watch you enjoy yourself," he said. "You light up the world when you're pleased."

She smiled back and touched his hand. "I'll never forget tonight," she said, "no matter what happens tomorrow."

"Tomorrow will be even better," he promised.

The waiter hovered near them, his face stern and sad over some problem of his own. Lili wished he would go away. But the restaurant had filled and people were waiting for tables. She knew that she and Kevin would soon have to leave.

"There will be other times," Kevin said, as though he had read her thoughts. "And the evening isn't over."

She thought she knew what he meant and loneliness tinged her desire. What if they never found their way back to the beach? She had been cold and contemptuous with Jim. What if something she said or did—or that Kevin said or did—made her freeze up again? She could imagine nothing more pitiful and grotesque than adultery turning sour, like a bad marriage, except that you would be left with not even legality.

The streets were crowded when they came out of the restaurant. People jostled each other on the sidewalk. Everyone seemed in a hurry, except Lili and Kevin. Neon lights blinked on and off, garish reminders of where they were and what they were doing. Half a dozen teenagers stood together at the corner. One of them whistled. Lili glanced at Kevin. He was smiling, untroubled by what had been implied. She was glad.

The car seemed another world. They sat in its isolation a while, not moving. She half-turned on the seat to see his face, which turned from purple to pink to rose to orange with the changing neons outside.

She moved close to him. They kissed. The kiss was a long one.

This was no transient attraction, she realized while their lips met. This would be for keeps, one way or another. Tonight there was passion and marvel—but the future could hold hurt. She had been married to a man with a skin like an elephant's. Kevin, she realized, could be injured by someone he loved. She would have to be careful, so very careful, always to be kind—

At last they moved apart.

"Kevin," she said gently.

"What?"

"You know."

"Yes."

Nothing else had to be said. He started the car and pulled into heavy traffic.

They drove for a long time through the thickening darkness, back the way they had come. Lili rested her head against his shoulder.

She opened her eyes when she heard the sound of

surf. The sky was a vast display of gift-wrapped stars. A cool breeze came through the window on Lili's side of the car to brush against her hair. Kevin was leaning forward, elbows on the steering wheel, a half-finished cigarette in his mouth. He turned and, in a look, entrusted her with all that he was.

He got out of the car. She heard his footsteps on gravel. They were parked near the office of a lonely seaside motel.

He returned with a key and started the car again. They drove past a row of cabins to the one which would be their own.

Inside the cabin, the sound of surf was intensified by the walls of the narrow room.

Lili stood quietly in the dark. He came up behind her, clasped his arms about her, just below her breasts. She could feel his desire as though it were part of herself—she could feel with his nerves, hope and fear with his breath. She turned in his arms, her mouth meeting his and once again she was lost in a flood of physical longing. His mouth enveloped hers as though they must consume each other, as if neither could be whole alone.

They rocked together in the middle of the dark room, the surf matching the beat of their blood. Never taking his mouth from hers, Kevin lifted her in his arms and carried her to the bed he had hired for them. Bedsprings creaked beneath the weight of their bodies.

She felt a vague fastidious distaste for her surroundings, followed by a savagely protective instinct to prevent any hurt to Kevin. For his sake, this grubby little motel must be the Taj Mahal. She had never reacted consistently to her husband even when she thought she loved him—she had asked herself, as though her concern had been with unknown weather, *Will I like it tonight—or will I wince at his touch?*

106

With Kevin, she had asked no questions. Whether or not he pleased her, she wanted Kevin to be pleased and reassured.

He must not think he had failed again at love. Above all else, she wanted him to be happy.

Ironically, as she forgot herself, her own self was returned to her. They clung together in nakedness and an ecstasy possessed her beyond her power of willing or pretense.

She had married partly for her ego's sake—Jim had been a good catch. She could never brag to friends about this night of motel love—but now she knew what the phrase meant, that life took on a meaning.

His body was heavy on hers, a shameful thing to be happening—and she silently gave him her canceled pride, her endurance of shame for love's sake, as a wedding gift between them in this mating that was not marriage.

"I love you," he whispered. "Love you, love you . . ."

The waves broke in the darkness.

At one point, Lili slept. She awoke in terror, not recognizing the unfamiliar bed at first nor the room nor even the man. Memory returned quickly, but the taste of terror lingered.

Kevin too had fallen asleep. He seemed to be having a bad dream. "Go home," he said to someone in his sleep. He lay on his side away from her, body tense even in a pose of relaxation, fists tight.

She leaned over him, hand on his shoulder. "You wouldn't mean me, would you?" she asked.

But he had forgotten her in his nightmare. He made small sounds of exasperation and anguish—and she listened, troubled for him and unable to reach or comfort him.

The waves were quieter, she thought—the low tide

point of the twenty-four hours must be quite close. She wondered what the actual time was and whether Jim had missed her—and what he would try to do to her when she returned.

Would there have to be real ugliness—perhaps tragedy? She didn't want the two men in her life fighting over her. She wanted no one hurt.

From another cabin, a sudden loud short cry intruded into the night. A cry of joy, pain, surprise— she would never know. The silence returned and the world was full of strangers with hidden sins and sorrows.

14

UNLIKE OTHER DREAMS, the war dream never had for Kevin the illusion of reality. Part of his mind always knew that what he saw were images out of the past. Only the motion was real.

There had been four of them—himself, Big Luke, Swartz, and Lane—sent out to make contact with the battalion on their left. The weather had been bitterly cold, with a steadily falling snow hiding the ravages of war throughout the countryside. Kevin, youngest of the four, had been in charge of the patrol. They had gone a mile when he knew something was wrong. The other battalion should have been within a half mile of their position. He had stopped the patrol in a small crevice of land and tried to think.

He closed his eyes; the memory was so vivid . . .

Big Luke, mustache flaked with snow, began his usual griping. "Where are those bastards hiding? We ain't got all day to sit and wait."

Swartz, owlish, small, and bitter, sat huddled against a bank of snow, his knees drawn to his chest. "It's cold enough to freeze the tits off—"

"Shut up," Big Luke snapped. "I've heard you say that a couple million times and I'm damned tired of it."

Swartz snorted obscenely.

Kevin and Lane exchanged glances. Lane was the man Kevin felt he could rely on. Lane, short and stocky, was a farmer from the wheat belt, where he had left a wife and two children. Lane had thought it his duty to enlist for a second round of war.

"Whatta we gonna do, Lieutenant?" Big Luke asked. He had a way of saying lieutenant that made it sound like a dirty word.

"We'll wait," Kevin answered. He had felt his youth more than he felt the cold.

"What the hell," Big Luke commented. "What for?"

"We'll wait," Kevin repeated.

He was conscious of angry looks from Big Luke and Swartz. They gave a damn chiefly about themselves, a point they had often made clear in the past. He knew they despised him, though he was not sure why. Sometimes he thought it was almost as if they imagined that they held him personally responsible for their presence in Korea, for the fact of war.

The soundless snow continued. Swartz seemed to have fallen asleep. Big Luke crouched like an angry cat, ready and willing to pounce on anything or anyone, friend or foe, who happened along. Lane sat Indian fashion, legs crossed, steel helmet beside him, rubbing his hand through his thinning dark hair. He was a good soldier who had received his baptism during World War II. He was overly cautious at times—at least by Kevin's young standards—yet he had never failed an assignment.

The minutes dragged. Nine-tenths of war, Kevin had learned, was waiting.

He moved near Lane. Snow peppered the farmer's hair, giving him a curiously sage-like look.

Lane asked, "You married, Lieutenant?"

"No."

"Funny how little we know about each other."

"Maybe it's better that way."

Lane put his helmet back on his head. "I miss my wife," he said. There was a plaintive note in his voice that Kevin had not heard before. In the four weeks they had been together he had never heard Lane complain. He was surprised and not pleased.

"All men miss their wives," he said uncomfortably, knowing his own ignorance.

"No, Lieutenant, that's not right. Swartz there is married and he don't give a hoot in hell about his wife. I hear him talk about her. All she means to him is a piece of flesh to be used as much as possible. A man like that don't really deserve a wife."

"We can't judge him, Lane. It's not for us to say."

"Why not, Lieutenant?" If Big Luke could make the title sound like an obscenity, Lane made it sound like a synonym for son.

Kevin tried to think of an answer, but there seemed none. He rubbed some snow across the sore knuckles on his left hand where he had accidentally skinned himself two days previously.

Lane went on, "My wife's the best woman in the world, Lieutenant. You know why? Because she's mine. She used to worry when we were younger, about her ankles. She thought they were thick. I told her I only like thick ankles on my women. Funny thing—once I said it, it was true."

Kevin did not understand exactly what Lane meant —he knew only that he had a sudden image of his mother and father being parted, which hurt and was not reasonable.

"Ever heard Swartz talk about his wife?" Lane went on. "He makes her out some kinda beauty queen. But he's not kidding anyone and that's a terrible thing. My wife and me, Lieutenant, we found something in each other, something more than most people ever find—" He turned his face to the white sky.

What he found there, Kevin would never learn.

They all heard the sound at the same time. Swartz was instantly awake, his eyes distorted. Big Luke

111

muttered a blasphemy with real feeling in it. Lane sighed, as though danger had turned monotonous and, for that reason alone, intolerable.

The sound came again—Chinese bugles. Kevin tried desperately not to believe what he knew instantly—that the sound came from behind them. They were cut off from their own battalion.

He motioned to Big Luke. "Get up on that ridge and take a look."

"Why me?"

"Because I say so," Kevin explained.

Big Luke scuttled away until he was only a vague shape through the falling snow. The others stood together, awaiting his return. The sound of bugles grew louder. Kevin felt like a ghost, haunting the slowly falling snow.

Big Luke was suddenly back. "There must be a million of the bastards," he said nastily. "We're up the creek without a paddle."

"No sense to this damned war," Swartz whined.

All three of them looked at Kevin, waiting for him to furnish their salvation. He knew there was only one thing he could do, under the circumstances—turn back to their battalion. Ahead, death was waiting.

They crept and crawled over the hills and through the gullies. A dense fog had suddenly come with the snow, helping to hide their movements. Twice the enemy passed them so close he could have touched skin. It took them the better part of two hours to go half a mile. For a while, Kevin thought they would make it without incident.

The sudden shot dug a hole in the snow scant inches from his elbow. More shots followed. He heard Big Luke yell out a curse and saw the big man stumbling through the snow, firing his rifle senselessly and uselessly in all directions. Slowly, like a puppet on a string, the soldier tilted over until he was on his knees and face, his anger at an end.

The three survivors dashed for a small embankment, tumbling over its edge while bullets spattered above their heads. Kevin heard a harsh grunt. Lane had been hit. The farmer rolled to the bottom of the embankment and stayed there, a shrunken ball of flesh and clothing. Swartz, surprisingly, had taken up a position and was methodically firing at shadows in the fog and snow.

Kevin had no idea how long they remained in the place, firing and reloading, firing and reloading . . .

Someone was shaking him by the shoulder and he recognized Captain Larkin and knew that everything was all right. He slid down the embankment and cradled Lane in his arms. The farmer was still alive. Blood stained his lips. His eyes, looking into Kevin's held a sure knowledge of death.

"My wife," Lane cried softly. The rest was a mumble of unintelligible sounds.

Kevin cried, unable to help himself, his face buried against the dead man's shoulder. When he looked up, he saw Swartz watching him with a curious pleased smirk, gloating that he was alive, that Big Luke and Lane had been the ones who died. Kevin was sick with shame at his own survival.

The dream world receded into more than a decade of yesterdays and Kevin returned to the present, conscious of Lili beside him. Many thousands of days had passed since Lane's death.

Lili said, "You've been awake for a long time."

"How did you know?"

"I just knew."

"How are you?"

"I'm fine, Kevin. I feel so alive it hurts. Is that a bad way to feel?"

113

"That depends," he said, "on how much it hurts. Let me look at you. I want to see your face."

He turned on a lamp beside the bed. In light, the room was small and tidy. The walls were blue, the simple furnishings in maple. An old print of Custer's Last Stand hung above a kneehole desk.

Lili touched his cheek. "You were far from me in the dark," she said.

"I was with a memory."

Lili looked stricken and he added quickly, "It had nothing to do with my ex-wife." He paused, wondering why the dream had chosen this night to return. He thought he knew. "I once knew a man who was deeply in love," he said. "He was in my platoon. A farmer from Minnesota. The last day he was alive, he told me how he loved his wife. After the war, I went to Minnesota to see her. She wasn't a pretty woman, in the way that you are, Lili. But it showed on her face that a good man had loved her. She was still—what's the word? Not proud, exactly—she was holy ground. This plain woman."

Lili shuddered with a kind of sympathy and moved close to him.

15

SHERI CAME OUT of the shower, rubbing herself briskly and efficiently with a soft towel. She hummed a melody to herself. She felt tired but happy. Her small, trim body, for all its toughness, ached to the very bone. Yet she felt better than she could remember feeling ever before in her life.

She was going to be as good as anyone else, with a man all her own, money and respectability. She would never have to hustle any more.

She walked naked into the other room. Sunlight flashed along the floor. Jim was sound asleep. She looked down at his wide forehead and blond hair. She had always felt reverence for costly and conspicious things—the good things, she called them—like mink and matched pearls. She felt the same reverence for Jim.

Laughing lightly, she began the process of dressing for the day. She touched herself lovingly, recalling the violence of his passion during the night, how demanding he had been, how wonderful . . .

She picked out her simplest dress. There was no longer a need for her to attract other men. One like Jim was enough. She turned to look at him once more, just before she left her cabin, and considered waking him up to come and have breakfast with her. She decided he needed the sleep, especially after last night.

The coffee shop was moderately crowded. Two

women whose acquaintance she had made were sitting in a booth. They beckoned for Sheri to join them. One was a tall brunette with a beautiful face, placid green eyes, and a body that was fifteen pounds too heavy. The other was short with an enormous bust and blond hair in a ponytail. Both were about thirty and, if Sheri remembered correctly, the brunette was currently involved with a divorce.

The brunette—her name was Grace—smiled knowingly as Sheri moved into the booth. She said, "We haven't seen much of you the last couple of days."

"I've been busy."

"We know." The sarcasm was not too subtle.

Sheri was too happy this morning to argue. "And what have you been doing with yourselves?"

Grace, her smile turning to a frown, replied, "Walking on the beach. Getting some exercise and sun."

The short, squat one giggled; her enormous bust jiggled with movement and she laid a heavy hand on Sheri's arm. "Exercise is good for the body and the soul."

"A man is better," Sheri said, unable to stop herself.

Grace made a sound that was almost obscene. "All men are fools, dear, a fact of life that you're old enough to know. Isn't that right, Barbara?"

Barbara giggled acknowledgement.

Sheri felt her happiness turning sour. She wished she had not joined the pair. They were a couple of freaks, she thought. She wondered if they were queer for each other.

Grace said, "I've seen you around with the blond guy."

Sheri was ravenously hungry. She kept looking for a waitress, but none was around.

"Isn't he married?" Grace kept prodding.

"Isn't who married?" Sheri said irritably.

116

Barbara laughed. "Listen to her."

Grace's smile was brittle. "Never mind, Barbara. Our little friend obviously prefers to keep her love life to herself. I can't say I blame her. Running around with a married man in a place like this—I must say, though, I feel sorry for his wife."

"Drop dead," Sheri suggested matter-of-factly.

"What?" Grace gasped. "What did you say?"

"Listen, you fat sow," Sheri explained in a controlled voice, "what I do is my own business. Keep your damned nose out of it. I can take one look at you and understand why your husband wants a divorce. There probably wasn't room enough for both of you in bed with all that extra weight you're carting around."

Grace's green eyes widened and her nostrils flared. "You've said enough, you cheap little whore."

"Language, language," Sheri chided.

"Everyone here has seen you parading around, half-naked, just wanting every man in the place to look at you and ogle you and—"

Sheri giggled, interrupting the tirade. "What's the matter? Jealous? Just because you're too fat to look decent in a swimsuit?"

"You're not being nice this morning, Sheri," Barbara said, giggling.

"You bore me, both of you," Sheri said.

She rose quickly and went outside, taking the path to the beach. She was sick with anger. What right did those ugly women have to sit in judgment on her? They had no right. They were all just like Jim's wife, all poured out of the same mold.

She stopped beneath a high palm, leaning against the trunk for support. Her mind was black and tortured. The mood was one which had been constant with her years earlier when she was a young girl

117

surrounded by a happy, virtuous, totally stifling family.

She had a right to Jim, she thought. He wanted her and she wanted him. It made no difference what she had been in the past, she had her life to live and if someone got hurt in the process, so much the better.

Boy, was she ever confused. Just a short time ago, she had been walking on clouds, sure that her life was going to change, that Jim was hers for keeps and all the rest a dream in the background. Those women had made her feel like scum scraped from the bottom of a barrel. Would Jim's friends be like those two? That could be worse than the life she was leading now. At least, until now, she had known where she stood.

With Sammy and Sammy's kind, she was good for one thing.

Jim's world would have different values. Could she fit in?

She walked back to the cabin, her morale sagging. She had touched a star and now the star was whizzing away, never perhaps to return. The real prize, she sensed dimly, was an inner one—her impulse to sing in the shower, for instance. As opposed to this blackness . . .

Jim was sitting on the edge of the bed in his shorts. His hair was mussed and his mouth was slack. He gave her a weak smile and shook his head. "I've never been this bushed before in my life," he said.

She tried to answer his smile. "A shower and some food will fix you up," she promised.

He looked at her as if trying to read her mind. "What's wrong?"

"Nothing."

"Come on, tell me."

"It's nothing, Jim, really."

He shrugged. "Have you had breakfast?"

118

"I . . . not yet."

"Where've you been?"

"Just for a walk."

"Where'd you get the energy?" His laughter was as weak as his smile had been.

She lit two cigarettes and handed him one. He accepted it avidly. In the light of morning, she saw the beginning of age around his mouth and eyes.

"What is it, Sheri?"

"I told you, nothing."

"Don't kid me. Something's happened. Have you seen my wife? Is that it?"

"No, Jim."

"Don't lie to me."

"I wouldn't lie to you."

He complained, "A great way to start the day."

She turned to the window. Two couples walked by in swimsuits, towels draped around their necks, laughing and talking, having a good time.

She asked, "What're your friends like, Jim? I mean, back home?"

"Like everyone else, I guess."

She turned and looked at him in anguish. "That's no answer."

"It's all the answer I can give you."

"Will they accept me? Will I fit in with them, Jim?" She tried to keep anxiety out of her voice.

"So that's it," he said. "I knew something was rubbing that little brain of yours the wrong way. You're worried about fitting in." He hesitated. "I grew up there, Sheri. I'm sort of a big cheese there. I have a house in a good neighborhood and my neighbors all respect me. Lili and I went around with a good crowd, but their morals are neither better nor worse than mine. You're a beautiful little dish with a cute wiggle behind you. The first month you're there, half my friends will make passes at you, just to see how

119

far they can get. I know, because I've made passes at their wives, and sometimes it works and sometimes it doesn't. That's the way of the world."

"Will they look down on me?"

"Why should they?"

"I'm not sure, Jim," she answered. "For the first time in my life, I'm frightened about myself."

His grin was almost mocking. "Want to back out?"

"I don't want to be unhappy, Jim. I don't think I could stand unhappiness."

"You think you'll find happiness with me?"

"That's just what I'm wondering about."

"Honey," he said with a knowing look, "you and I fit into a certain mold. Let's face it. We both like it and we know how to do it. We're a couple of old pros between the sheets. There's nothing wrong with admitting what we are. So we'll spend the next few years bedding each other as many times as possible. And then—" he shrugged, not finishing.

"And then what?"

"Who knows?"

"I want to know right now."

"Okay," he said. "Then, I'll probably start worrying about you. I'll go downhill faster than you. Sooner or later, a time will come when old Jim Thompson will no longer give you what you want. That's the time when you'll start searching around for someone to help you through the long nights—"

"Brother," she interrupted, "you're a cynical bastard."

"No, merely a realist. I've seen it happen often enough. My own boss is only in his mid-forties. But his wife is ten years younger and she tells me he's like a dishrag most of the time. He knows she sneaks around behind his back. What he doesn't know is with whom."

Listening to him, Sheri felt her black mood fade

to a blue one. Maybe there was no real difference between his world and hers, which was reassuring. Yet she wished there were respectability and decency in the world and that she could possess them. Jim made them sound like myths—the true facts were vicious. She realized that men would still be pawing at her, desiring her, even if she were married.

"Does your wife fit in?" she asked.

"Lili?" He laughed. "I suppose, since she's beautiful, that a few of my friends tried to get to first base with her. I doubt if any of them made it."

"That's not what I meant," Sheri said. "I meant—well, she knows how to dress and entertain and—"

"Honey," he interrupted her, "don't worry about that part of it. You'll fit in. You'll be invited to all the parties and you'll join the Thursday bridge club and find the usual stupid little errands to get involved with. You'll be my wife."

She liked the sound of the words. Suddenly, her apprehensions seemed childish. She would make them accept her, like her, in the way she had always achieved her ends—by going after what she wanted, by being herself.

16

LILI FELT THE STUBBLE of morning beard on her lover's face. Daylight had come. She realized that she had done a drastic thing. What would Jim do to her for staying away all night? Curiously, what she found in herself was not fear but wistfulness, as though she had to leave a party too early. Dying young was rather like cutting short a vacation.

Kevin said, "Are you hungry?"

"I'd like some coffee," she said.

He laughed lightly, stirring away from her. His mood, she realized, was a happy one. He went to the window and peered through the curtains.

"It's another bright day," he said.

"Good." Her tone was approving. In the morning light, God help her, she was being polite and civilized, as though she and Kevin had just met at the home of a friend.

He turned to look at her, rubbing a hand along his face. "We don't get much sun in San Francisco."

"I'm sure the Chamber of Commerce wouldn't like to hear you saying that."

"We have other things," he said. "Someone once described San Francisco as an old lady looking back on a rowdy past."

"I've been there."

"Visiting there and living there are two different things. You'll love it, believe me."

"Am I going to live there?"

"Where else?"

She uttered a pleasant laugh. "I love you, Kevin. I love you so much that if I were standing up now, my knees would be shaking."

"I like you better lying down."

"You're a nut," she said. "I wish we could stay here, though. This place is sort of nowhere, no city at all."

"I thought you wanted coffee."

The condemned woman, she thought, drank a hearty breakfast. "You're terribly logical," she said. "Is that because you're a lawyer?"

He returned to the bed and sat beside her, reaching for her hand. "The law has nothing to do with logic," he explained. "They're poles apart. That was one of my troubles when I first started law school. I tried to apply the rules of logic to law. Logic is uncluttered. Law is complex."

"Are you a good lawyer, Kevin?"

"I will be, eventually. Right now, I'm still learning." He frowned thoughtfully. She sensed that he wanted to build a basis of understanding and trust between them.

He wanted it almost too obviously.

He knew they had been strangers when yesterday's sun came up, yet now they were sitting close to each other, without a stitch of clothing on, talking calmly. Something she never could have done with Jim, she thought fleetingly.

"My work is important to me, Lili," he went on. "I hope you realize that."

She suppressed a tender desire to laugh.

"A man's work should be important to him," she said. The basis of understanding and trust, she thought with pride and loneliness and love, would be a little one-sided, consisting of her understanding of Kevin—and Kevin's trust in her. She would not be the one who was understood—who would put herself, with childlike trust, into someone else's keeping.

"Felice couldn't understand that."

"Felice?"

"My ex-wife."

"Did she give you a very bad time?"

"She was a bum," he said. "Today I can tell you that, without feeling torn in pieces. Yesterday it killed me. You're wonderful for me, Lili."

"Are you sure," she asked, "that you don't think I'm a bum too?"

He looked shocked, almost hostile. "Because you're here with me? The thing between us is beautiful. To me, you're practically a saint."

But she was no saint to her own way of thinking. Adultery was adultery, no matter how beautiful.

She would have to carry the guilt, she realized dispassionately, both for Kevin and herself. Kevin was wonderful—and she had fallen in love with him—but he was not strong enough for guilt. Maybe no one was—a fact she might be on the verge of learning.

She watched him go into the bathroom for a shower. She had no inkling of his likes and dislikes in the ordinary little things of everyday living, like his preference in toothpaste. It took time for people to become acquainted with each other's habits and tastes —but in the important ways, like what they could mean to one another, there was instant recognition. She and Kevin had met under impossible conditions, yet their meeting had changed the future.

She should not question good fortune or happiness, she thought. She had spent a long time searching for them and now that she had them, why torment herself with guilt?

Perhaps no one could choose his torments—perhaps that was the price you paid for freedom to choose your joys. She thought of her home, her friends and family, all the familiar surroundings.

One way or another, all of them were behind her.

But what if things were as they seemed? What if Kevin, who loved her, brought her paradise on a platter for the rest of her days?

They were good together, in more ways than one.

Why must she question their right to live?

She tossed on the pillow, angry at herself. She looked down at her naked body and remembered the wonder of their love-making in the night. She put her hands against her breasts and recalled the touch of his lips, his fingers, so unlike any experience she had known before . . .

The shower ceased and Kevin came into the room, rubbing a towel through his hair, a broad smile on his face. "I'm ready for anything now," he said.

"Anything?"

"You heard me right."

She laughed and he threw the still damp towel at her. She caught it, savored its faint odor of soap. He's a morning sort of person, she thought—no hangover, no grouch. She wondered how many mornings they would actually share. Perhaps this moment was no more than a window into a world that might have been—a house that might never be built.

"What is it?" he asked quickly. He had put on his shorts and T-shirt. "You're frowning."

"Am I?"

"A beautiful woman should never frown in the morning."

She laughed. "I agree with you."

"See that you do, always," he answered.

"Is this your true self? Are you always so happy and full of life?"

"Always," he said again. "You have a big treat ahead, getting really to know me." He had put on his shirt and slacks and he stood with hands at his sides, looking at Lili with a tender cocksureness that touched her. "I thought we covered some of the salient features. What more would you like to know?"

"So many different things."

"Name one."

"Let me think," she said, trying to sound frivolous as she lay nude in daylight, totally visible to him. "Are you handy at cooking and cleaning?"

"No, I don't think so. I'm a genius with little children, though, and elderly ladies. Ask more questions."

"You're not making it easy for me, Kevin."

"I don't intend to," he said with that special little smile of his, the one she was getting to know. His eyes crinkled at the corners when he smiled like that and he had just the barest hint of a dimple in his left cheek.

"Kevin, am I beautiful? Really?" She stirred on the bed.

"A nonsensical question," he answered.

"Tell me."

"You're beautiful, Lili. You're beautiful and ravishing and your curves curve in the right places and your hips are rounded the right way, to fit just between my two hands, and your breasts are the color of new-fallen snow and your nipples look like berries in July."

"That's what you see when you look at me?"

"That's what I see. And if I keep it up, thinking about you, looking at you, I'm liable to get undressed again, and then—"

"You're so good for me, Kevin. You and your talk. And your kisses."

"Didn't you know?" he asked jokingly. "I'm ol' Doc Morris, the man with the sure-fire cure for all women, regardless of age or color or weight."

"Mrs. Kevin Morris," she said idly. "It has a nice sound."

126

She flung one arm out, so that her breasts were high and the marks of the beating Jim had given her, so few hours ago, were clearly visible. Now, surely, Kevin would notice, would ask questions—

He came to the edge of the bed, stooped over and pulled the blankets around her. "There," he said, "that's better. You're too damned beautiful. When I look at you like that, I want you again and again—and I don't want you getting tired of me."

"Kiss me," she said lightly. Now she had her answer. She would carry the punishment alone, whatever it proved to be.

His kiss was sweet and full of reassurance. She felt the pull of passion within her once more and fought against it. Too much passion could add up to a lie.

"I'll tell you about me," he said, sitting down beside her. "I was born a long time ago and I was a spoiled brat. My parents gave me everything I wanted. I had my first woman when I was eight and I'm a ring-tailed wonder who growls when he doesn't get his way. I'm sarcastic and vindictive and I get drunk every two or three days and, on the side, I pimp for the fanciest whorehouses in all of San Francisco, and—"

"And you're the biggest liar this side of Hades."

"And I'm the biggest liar this side of Hades," he agreed. "Lili," he went on, looking at her carefully, "do you want me to talk a little about my first marriage?"

"Only if you feel it does you good."

"I owe it to you," he said and she knew he wanted to talk, "to tell you all about Felice. I'm not a man, you understand, who has a quarrel with life."

"I understand," she said.

"But I see so much that hurts me. I ache when I feel pity—I bleed. Can't help it. Take the war. I was

127

there and I suppose I came back more of a man than when I went in. I don't know. How do you measure such things? I had to kill and if that makes me more of a man, then okay, that's it. I didn't like it. I'll never be able to understand why there have to be things like war. Yet my existence as a lawyer depends upon minor wars, wars between human beings instead of countries. I know that no shooting is involved. But the people who get forced into courtrooms are often as deeply scarred by what happens to them as any front-line soldier.

"And then," he continued, "there was my wife. I thought I had found some kind of refuge with her. Yet life with Felice turned out more of a nightmare than anything else I've ever experienced. Don't get me wrong—I'm not trying to place the blame on her entirely. She couldn't help what she was. Did I tell you once before that she was mentally ill? The psychiatrist gave me a pat on the back and a mouthful of meaningless words which didn't help in the least. It was just a situation, like the war, and I had to make the best of it. Maybe I chickened out on her. I don't know. I know I woke up one morning when I couldn't take any more from her." He smiled affectionately. "Now, do you know enough about me?"

"I know I love you," she said in a small voice.

"And is that enough?" At last he sounded humble.

"It has to be, Kevin."

"Good," he said. He rose, stretching his arms above his head, stifling a yawn. "I feel the need of some morning air. When I get back, I expect to see you showered and dressed, and then we'll feed these empty stomachs of ours."

"Is that an order?"

"It sure is," he said.

She blew a kiss at him as he went out the door.

Last night he had spoken of taking her from

danger, even out of the country. The warm love bed had gentled all his fears.

She felt at peace with herself as she rose from bed. No matter what else happened, she had known a capsule lifetime—she had been given a gift of love, a kind of Pandora's box with her lover's weakness and strength, wisdom and blindness, all mixed together.

She was a bride . . .

Kevin watched the seagulls floating inches above the waves. Some small boys were splashing and yelling along the edge of the beach. Farther out, a motorboat skimmed across the water with a muscular water-skier following in its wake. A dozen or so nut-brown bodies lay in the sand, soaking up morning sun.

He was overflowingly happy. Everything looked good to him. What great day was this—why didn't everyone shout with joy?

He heard the urgent screech of rubber against pavement. A car loaded with teenagers careened into the parking lot. Almost before the car stopped, golden bodies were leaping across the sand and toward the water.

He looked back at the motel where he had spent the night. He could barely see their cabin through the high screen of shrubbery. Had Lili risen? He visualized her standing beneath the shower spray, the rivulets of water coursing down that lovely body, touching her where he had touched her during the night, following the same routes that he had followed.

He was a man in love, he appraised himself, and his brain was reeling with the wonder of it all.

He knew, looking at it from this distance, that the motel would be shoddy in another year or so. But last night the cabin had been a shrine of love.

He had been unable to wait any longer last night. His desire for Lili had reached an unbearable intensity and he had stopped at the first possible place. Now the shoddy, rambling motel would be a memory for both of them to share. They would have much to share in the future.

An old man, with brittle-looking shoulders, ambled up to Kevin. The old man's eyes were intent and bright as he watched the tanned young bodies on the beach. "A spectacle," he said in a strained voice.

"A what?" Kevin asked.

"A spectacle," the old man repeated. "Those young girls running around with hardly any clothes on. Not decent."

Kevin said, "They're nice, though." Today, there was no evil—not even in an old man's mind.

"In my day and age," the ancient went on, "they'd all be locked up and the key thrown away." His gaze remained greedily on the suntanned figures. "Fools, all of 'em." His hands clenched and unclenched shakily. "Hell's fire, it's just not decent. They give an old man bad thoughts and such thoughts are for the young, the very young. Right?"

"Bad thoughts are nice," Kevin said largely.

"They tease those young boys," the old man continued. "They tease 'em and drive 'em to distraction. They shouldn't do that. Man is born of woman and then woman turns around and teases him the rest of his life. They shouldn't be allowed to run around with next to nothing on. They're nasty, those little girls."

"Maybe it's you that's nasty, old man," Kevin said.

The old man cackled unpleasantly. "Sure, boy, you hit the nail right on the head. It's me all right. You're a smart boy. Not many boys'd tell that to an old man. Smart and honest, that's you, huh? Don't ever get old, boy. Die when you still got it and then you'll

130

never know the torments an old man goes through."

Kevin found he could no longer reconcile his brittle companion's existence with the goodness of the day. He turned without another word and walked away. Today he could not absorb a single unpleasant fact. He followed the shoulder of the highway back to the motel cabins. Two heavy-set men were standing in front of the manager's office, apparently engaged in argument. They stopped talking to look at him.

"Good morning," he greeted them both.

One of them asked, "What happened to you, brother? You just find a million bucks?"

Lili was dressed and standing by the window, a smile of welcome on her face. "I was watching you," she said. "You look so happy, Kevin. There ought to be a way of bottling some of the air around you. For later use, you know. In case someone gets a grouch."

"I've been philosophizing with the natives," he accounted for himself, putting his arm across her shoulders tenderly.

"Do I pass inspection?"

He held her at arm's length, pretending critical scrutiny. Her face was scrubbed and fresh-looking. The only make-up she wore was a bright shade of lipstick. Her eyes were untroubled and kind. The skirt and sweater and low-heeled shoes, which she had worn last night, looked even better this morning. Her ash-blond hair was a mist about her face.

"You'll do," he said, "in a pinch."

She was in his arms. He could feel the curves of her body blending into his and, momentarily, he wished they were still in bed. He liked the thought, though, that she was different from Felice, who always wanted to be in bed.

They walked outside arm in arm. She paused in front of the cabin, looking around her, as if trying to memorize each detail of her surroundings. "I'll never forget this place," she said. It struck him that her voice was firm. He wondered why firmness was called for.

They sat in the car in silence, as if each were reluctant to leave. Lili said matter-of-factly, "Kevin, I've never done that before—spent the night with a man other than my husband."

"You didn't have to tell me that."

"I wanted you to be sure."

"It wouldn't make any difference, Lili, one way or the other. I love you for yourself, not your past or lack of past." He knew he was sincere. His life had begun anew and whatever had happened before mattered little or nothing now. "Our lives began the other night on the beach. Whatever came before with either of us is inconsequential. We have the present, Lili, you and I together, and the promise of the future. There is no past."

"No past," she echoed. "You're sure?"

"None that counts."

She smiled, placing her hand on his arm. "This is daylight," she said. "I have to be a realist, Kevin. We're not hiding beneath the blankets now. For you the operation has already been accomplished. You're divorced and the scar is healing. For me, the operation is just beginning. I have to go back and tell Jim—" she shrugged helplessly—"I'm not sure what I can tell him. That part may be up to Jim."

"I'll go with you," he said. "We'll tell him together."

She shook her head. "I can't have that," she said. "I won't do that to him."

"You can't mean you still care for him," Kevin exclaimed with a faint sense of fear.

"No, Kevin. I mean I had a contract with him—as you did with Felice. And there's such a thing as a courageous break—instead of a sniveling one. If I let you come with me, if I let you accept part of my burden now, I just won't think of myself as a person any more. Pamper me in this one thing, Kevin, please."

He was silent for a while, driving down the road toward breakfast. He felt pleased with Lili's principles—yet remembering Jim in rage, he was afraid for Lili.

But facing Jim alone seemed important to her. After all, he reasoned, the man had to be rational— he held a job, he drove a car.

"Kevin, please," she said again. "Say it's all right."

He nodded slowly. "If it's what you want."

"I've told you that."

"All right," he said.

"Thank you. It means a lot to me." She smiled cheerfully. "And now let's get something to eat. I'm famished."

He asked, "Are you going to tell him today?"

"Maybe not today," she murmured. "I don't want this day spoiled, you see. I want to spend the whole day with you, doing whatever comes into our heads. I don't think I want to go back just yet."

He thought quickly. "But there's the fact that you were out all night. Won't he—"

"He won't worry, Kevin, believe me. He won't concern himself over me until he sees me."

"If you say so," he said. He was not entirely satisfied with their program but, as she had pointed out, today was the one treasure they had. Nothing must be permitted to cloud this perfect day.

17

Jim blew smoke into Sheri's face, laughing mirthlessly.

She made an odd sound and waved her hands before her face.

"You're just a great big playful boy, aren't you?" she said sarcastically.

"What's the matter? You unhappy with the service?"

She managed a laugh. The honey-haired waitress looked at them from the counter as if she could not understand why anyone was laughing so early in the morning.

"You're my kind of guy, sweetie," Sheri said.

"Hell, who you trying to kid?" he asked, unable to keep the sneering tone out of his voice. "Any guy's your kind of guy. If it hadn't been me these last couple of days, it would have been some other jerk. I know your kind, honey, and all you want is some guy with enough energy and know-how to make you happy between the sheets."

"Cut it out, Jim," she said between clenched teeth.

He took another drag on the cigarette. I'm a great guy, he thought. I sure am. Just a short while ago, I was building her up and now I'm trying to tear her down. What's with me?

What the hell's wrong with me?

In a way, he knew. He had gone back to his cabin this morning. Lili had not been there. There was no evidence of her having been there through the night either and, in changing his clothes, he discovered that his car keys were gone. Where the hell was she? He thought of her spending the night with that man she had picked up in the bar. The little bitch, he kept thinking incredulously.

"Are you mad at me, or something?" Sheri asked.

"Why should I be mad at you?"

"I don't know. You're acting kind of funny, that's all."

"I'm acting like myself," he growled.

They were silent while the waitress refilled their coffee cups. He watched the waitress moving away, the cute little wiggle of her fanny. He groaned inwardly. He was sacked, bushed, beaten, yet he still had to make an effort to be himself, to look and stare and goggle, and let the world know what a great lover he was.

He wondered about Lili. He could not understand her. She would never again get under his hide, not any more. But she was a possession of his and the thought of her running around was a thorn in his side. It was inconceivable to him that she could prefer someone else when she could have had Jim Thompson. He had expected to find her in the cabin, cowering and ready to do anything he wished. Instead she had probably spent the whole night with a stranger.

"What was that guy's name?" he asked abruptly.

"What guy?"

"You know, the one on the tennis court yesterday."

She stared at him craftily. "Kevin Morris?"

"You know which cabin he's in?"

"How would I know that?"

A dull throbbing persisted in the back of his head. He studied Sheri. She appeared small and fragile. Yet he knew how violent she could be at times, how stormy and demanding. Why should he be concerned

135

with a bitch like Lili when he had someone like Sheri to satisfy him? There was no sense in his worrying. He and Lili had never had the real thing between them, at least not as far as he was concerned. He just could not stand the thought of her turning away from him. It had to be the other way around. No woman walked out on Jim Thompson.

"What's wrong, Jim?" Sheri interrupted his thoughts.

"Nothing. Quit nagging me."

"I wasn't nagging you. I was just—"

"For the love of Mike, will you shut up!"

Her eyes narrowed to angry slits and, slowly, she straightened up in her seat. "I don't want you talking to me like that, Jim," she said in a tight voice. "I don't like it."

"That's too damned bad."

She rose stiffly, distaste in her face. "When you get in a better mood," she said, "I'll be in my cabin."

"Alone?" He could not resist the dig.

"Damn you, Jim. Damn you to hell." Her tears felt hot and helpless. "What's gotten into you?"

He shook his head, trying not to look at her. "Go ahead. I'll see you later."

"Just like that, huh?"

"Just like that, baby."

"You turn it on and off pretty damned quick."

"Part of my charm."

He thought she was going to say something else, but she merely straightened her shoulders, turned and walked quickly out of the dining room.

He was alone. It seemed to him that he almost never had time alone any more. It was nice just to sit by himself for a change. He tried to make his mind a blank, not to think of anything at all.

When he did that, sense usually came to fill the vacuum.

He was born to be busy. He and Lili led a busy social life, something he wanted. It was important to him to see people, to be a vital part of the world around him. When had he last had time alone? He could not remember. The bank kept him busy, more than busy. He knew what they thought of him at the bank. He could charm the customers with his handsome smile. He had been a big football star in college. Such things counted in his business. Mack Allen was pushing him along. There were big things in store for his future and, for a moment, he wondered how that future would be affected if he brought someone like Sheri home with him. She was worried about fitting in and she had reason.

She was certainly no great intellect and she had none of the social graces that Lili had. Sheri had that cute little motion and that talent in bed and that was the end of it.

He could see them all now, drooling over her, trying to get her into the sack with them. He knew his friends, damn them—their trouble was that they were all just like himself, thinking about sex all the time, and how could he trust Sheri in a situation like that? It would never do for him to be laughed at. No one ever laughed at Jim Thompson.

The waitress was standing above him. "Anything else this morning, sir?" she asked with a brilliant smile.

"What did you have in mind?" He could not help himself—he had to make the effort.

"Mister," she said, "I get off at four."

"Fine. We'll see about it."

"You get right to the point, don't you?"

"Why not?" He laughed.

She dropped the check on the table and swished her hips sensually as she turned and left. She looked pert and enjoyable. She could be another milestone in his long search for satisfaction.

When the hell would he learn? He could not keep going like this. Yet he gave her a broad wink and a smile as he rose, leaving too large a tip. It never paid to ignore anything, especially in skirts.

He walked out, his mind returning to Lili, a dull anger backing up within him, like a clogged pipeline. She had no right to be treating him like this and he was going to make her pay. Damn right. No one made a fool out of Jim Thompson, not even his wife.

Sheri was seething with anger. She stood in the bright sunlight and thought of how stupidly she had behaved with Jim. She had let him get her goat. She still wanted to go back and slap his foolish, handsome face. Who did he think he was, treating her like a joke. She was okay with Jim when he had her between the sheets. Then, everything was lovey-dovey, a world of promises. But get him out in the daylight —after he had what he wanted—and he was something else again, teasing her, tormenting her.

Hell with him.

She had only been fooling herself with her dreams. She should have known better.

She walked stiffly along the pathway toward her cabin, desperately trying to think of a way to get back at him. She wasn't going to let him get away with humiliating her, not by a long shot. No one was going to take Sheri for a ride.

She opened the door and stopped in amazement, one hand going to her throat. "Oh, no," she exclaimed.

The man in the chair gave her a smile. She knew what his expression really betokened and she was frightened.

He said, "Hello, Sheri."

"Sammy!"

"I had a hard time finding you, baby. You've caused me a lot of trouble and a lot of money."

She searched her thoughts for the right words to say to him. There seemed none. Nor did he help her.

He sat like a coiled cobra, smiling that evil smile, his eyes piercingly bright, his hands calm on the arms of the chair. He was wearing a brown suit and matching tie. The tie was held in place by a gold tie-clasp. He slowly removed the tie-clasp and held it between his fingers. He looked up from the clasp to Sheri's face.

"Remember when you gave me this, baby?" he asked.

"Sure, honey," she answered, moving slowly across the room, watching him carefully. This was not like Sammy. He should have been furious with her by now.

"It was at Lake Mio, a year ago." He twisted the metal between his fingers. "You surprised me that night, baby. I didn't think you were sentimental enough to go out and buy me a present. You touched me." His smile grew frankly sinister. "I thought maybe we had something going for us." He leaned forward, hands on his knees. "What the hell did you run away for, Sheri? Wasn't I good to you? Didn't I give you what you wanted?"

She wasn't sure she was hearing correctly. Could there be a pleading tone in Sammy's voice? What was wrong? He just wasn't acting as Sammy was supposed to.

"Sammy," she said, "I'm sorry. I had to get away."

"But why?"

"I was tired, that's all."

He rose and moved toward her. His strong fingers dug into the flesh of her shoulder.

139

She looked up into his face. "You're hurting me, Sammy."

"Am I?" He twisted her flesh more roughly. "You ran out on me, baby. For the first time in my life, I missed someone. Can you understand that? I never thought it would happen to me. I'm a wise guy. I know all the answers. But when you skipped out on me—" he shook his head, taking his hand from her shoulder—"I had to find you, baby. That was all there was to it."

"What are you trying to tell me?"

"Do I have to spell it out for you? You want me to crawl?"

A bubble of excitement formed in her stomach and burst through her. She laughed. This was good, real good. Imagine. Tough-guy Sammy, wise-guy Sammy. If she were not actually living this she would not believe it. "Yes," she said, feeling a new-found power within her, "you have to spell it out for me, Sammy. You have to tell me what you mean."

He slapped his hands together, muttering agonizedly. She watched him joyously, the existence of Jim Thompson slipping from her mind.

"Okay," Sammy said. "Okay."

"Okay what?"

"I want you back, and that's it."

"How back, Sammy?"

"What do you mean?"

"You know what I mean, you weasel you. Do you want me back like it was, fleecing those fat old men? Is that what you want?"

He shook his head sadly. "Don't kick me when I'm down, baby."

"Why shouldn't I?"

He exploded, "The life wasn't so bad, was it? We lived pretty high on the hog, didn't we? What right

140

have you got to complain? Hell, I found you when you were grubbing for pennies. I turned you—"

"You turned me into a high-priced whore, and that's all," she interrupted.

"So what's wrong with that?"

"I'm finished with it," she said. "I don't want that kind of life any more. I've had it. No more fat old men with blubbery stomachs, panting for air like they were going to drop dead from a heart attack. No sir. I've had it."

He eyed her craftily. "You got something lined up here, is that it?"

She hesitated, then decided there was no sense in lying to him. "I thought I did," she said. "I thought I had me a real, first-class sucker on the line, but he turned sour on me."

Sammy laughed. His laugh was magnificent. He threw back his head and guffawed, slapping his sides. "That's a good one, a damned good one. Little Sheri couldn't make it on her own. Ah, baby, come on back with me." He was serious now, intently so. "Come on. I'm asking you nice-like. We had good times together, big times, and we've got a lot of living to do before these old bones give out."

"Maybe you didn't hear me right, Sammy," she said. "I'm not going back to those fat old men. No more of that for this little girl."

"You're serious, aren't you?"

"Never more so."

"Okay, baby, on your terms. Just the two of us. I'm not sure old Sammy can remain honest and at the same time keep the wolf from the door, but we'll give it a try."

"Why, Sammy." She ran across the room into his arms. She gave him a soft kiss and buried her head in the niche of his shoulder, hugging him with all her strength. The thought crossed her mind that going

141

back to Sammy would be sweet revenge on Jim, who had insulted her.

All that jazz about respectability and decency was for the birds. Sheri did not belong with someone like Jim. She belonged right here where she was—Sammy was her kind and she was his.

He held her a little away from him, looking into her eyes, "How about this sucker you lined up? Can we make a thin dime on him, just to cover expenses?"

"I don't think so." She paused. "I'd rather not, Sammy."

"Serious, huh?"

"I thought it might be."

Sammy's grin was friendly. "Let me guess, baby," he said. "The guy's probably around thirty or so, tall and handsome, and he's got a good job back home. He fed you a line about taking you back to a vine-covered cottage and making a respectable woman out of you."

She winced painfully. "You're not far wrong, honey."

Sammy laughed bitterly. "Baby, you've still got some growing up to do. You're not dry behind the ears. You get away from old Sammy for a couple of weeks and you fall for the oldest line in the books."

"Maybe," she said. She heard her door opening and turned to see Jim Thompson. "Well," she said, "and a good morning to you, big man."

Jim's face was dark with anger. He stared at Sammy. "Who's this guy?"

"What difference does that make?"

"I asked you a question."

"Take it easy, friend," Sammy said softly. "I'd suggest that you turn around and go home. Your fun's over for now."

"Is it?" Jim growled. He took a couple of steps toward Sammy.

142

Sheri was not sure what happened next. Suddenly the two men were close and then Sammy was falling backwards. He hit the floor with a dull thump and lay there blinking his eyes. A grimace of pain distorted his face.

"Damn you," she snapped at Jim.

He looked at her uncomprehendingly. "Sheri," he said.

"Get out, you big ape," she screamed at him. "Get lost."

His eyes narrowed angrily. She thought he was going to strike her and then, slowly, he shook his head and made an obscene sound with his lips.

"A two-bit whore," he snarled. "Just a lousy two-bit whore."

She was no longer interested in his opinion of her or anything else. She sank to her knees and lifted Sammy's head to her lap, cradling his head as a mother might do to a hurt child.

She should have known better, she thought, than to dream of abandoning Sammy.

Jim was standing above them. He seemed to be talking to himself. She could not make out his words. He shoved a hand into his pocket and a dollar bill floated to the floor. She finally made out what he was saying.

"Is that what you usually get, a buck a throw?"

"You lousy bastard," she said.

Sammy groaned and tried to get up but she held him tightly.

"I always pay my whores," Jim insisted. "Pick up the money."

"Drop dead," she suggested.

She knew that he was having a hard time controlling himself, knowing that she was playing with fire by inviting his temper—yet, strangely, she didn't care. She only wanted him out of her cabin so she

143

could be alone with Sammy. Nothing else seemed as important.

"You take chances," Jim snarled.

Sammy groaned again.

She said to Jim, "Go back to your wife."

A change came over him. She could read the sudden tightening around his mouth before he slapped her cheek and sent her reeling across the floor.

When she could focus again, she saw that he was making to grab Sammy by the collar. She screamed and Jim glanced at her, loosening his hold on Sammy. He stood poised, bent at the waist, an animal ready to spring on its prey. Then he made a growling sound in his throat and ran out of the cabin, slamming the door behind him.

She crawled toward Sammy. He was grinning weakly. He had managed to right himself to a sitting position and was rubbing his temples with his fingertips. His eyes were as venomous as a snake's.

"No, Sammy," she said. "Whatever you're thinking—no."

He stopped rubbing his temples. His grin was still weak. He said, "I'll kill him, baby." His tone of voice was utterly calm, utterly deadly.

"Honey, it wouldn't do any good. Don't think about him."

"Easy to say."

"Sammy—please."

He reached for a chair, pulling himself to his feet. He helped her to rise and slowly lighted a cigarette.

"Sammy," she said.

"Nobody gets away with roughing me up like that," he said.

"What good would it do to tangle with him again?"

"Satisfaction, baby. Good old satisfaction."

"And the cops would be here and—Sammy, you mustn't even think about it. You said before, we've still got living to do. There's no sense in spoiling everything just because some big monkey knocked you around."

"Isn't there?"

"You know there isn't."

He paced the room, followed by a little cloud of smoke. She was responsible, she thought. All this was her fault. Damn it, why hadn't she known when she had a good thing going for her?

She said, "Come on, sweetie. Let me pack up and we'll shake out of here."

He paused and said in a monotone, "Baby, when you pick 'em, you really pick 'em. That guy packs a punch like a mule's kick. He rubbed a hand across his jaw. "Haven't I always told you not to mess with the big young ones? They're trouble from the word go, believe me. Hell, you can't make a living that way."

She went to him and hugged him tightly. "Oh, sweetie," she murmured. "Everything's okay now, isn't it?"

"Sure," he said.

"And it'll be just like it was with us before, won't it?"

"Whatever you say, baby." He vouchsafed her a slyly triumphant smile. "I've never been to Honolulu —now that you're talking sense again, how about us going there? The pickings ought to be pretty ripe, with all the tourists coming in."

"Anything you say, Sammy." She hugged him tighter.

She belonged with him. They would make it, the two of them, no matter what it cost her.

18

JIM SAT CAREFULLY in the chair, nursing the bottle. He had drunk the better part of it in some three hours, yet his head was sparklingly clear. His thoughts were all in order. He knew what he was going to do. No one had ever made a fool of him before, and now there were two of them, one a cheap little hustler and the other his wife.

Okay.

He smiled grimly, steadied himself and took another short drink. Easy, boy, he told himself—don't gulp. Don't pass out. Be prepared. Afternoon sun slanted through the opened blinds, a brilliant splash on the blue carpeting.

He'd show them, he thought. He'd show the little bitches what kind of a man Jim Thompson was. No one was going to hustle him, play him for a sucker.

What a sour world. He couldn't fathom what had happened to him. First, his wife, and now a common little whore. The anger grew like a giant twin within him, giving him added strength, even a sense of companionship. He wanted to lash out at something, anything, and he was finding it hard just to sit there, waiting and waiting.

When would she come back? He relished the thought of seeing her walk through that doorway. He would teach her a good lesson this time—apparently, last time had not been enough for her. Well, this time would be—he would see to it, damn right he would.

Imagine her, stepping out with some other bastard and never even giving him the time of day. How many times had he looked into her eyes and seen only loathing? How many times had she been cold, barely moved by him, just wanting to get through it? Who the hell did she think she was?

Absently, he took another drink from the bottle, holding it in his mouth before swallowing. Revenge. He was going to get his revenge, but good. Wonderful just to sit there and think about what he would do to her. She had her high stinking morals, telling him all the time what was wrong with him, telling him not to chase around. And now look at them. He wondered if she had been pulling the wool over his eyes all along, making a fool out of him behind his back. If she had—how many people were laughing at him back home?

He kept watching the door.

He had all the time in the world. He was going to wait if it took the rest of his life.

He'd show them, damn them.

Lili would be the example.

He took another drink. He might have to phone the desk, have them send another bottle. That was all right. They had plenty of bottles, just as he had plenty of time.

Kevin drove carefully through congested traffic, occasionally glancing at Lili beside him. She had curled up with her head against the back of the seat and seemed asleep. Passing lights helped him stay wakeful.

He felt a pang of doubt when they reached the coast highway and turned north. They would soon be at the motel where they had first met.

How would Lili make out, facing her husband?

147

Everything had to turn out all right, he kept insisting to himself. He might remain in the background, but he would still be within hearing distance, after he and Lili parted at the end of the trip.

The day had been long and wonderful. They had returned to Los Angeles after breakfast, had been the first visitors when the zoo opened in Griffith Park. They had taken the long, circular walk around the zoo, watching and feeding the animals, holding hands and talking. They had lunched on hot dogs and root beer, had watched a kids' baseball game.

A golden, glorious day.

She had told him about her childhood, about the crush she had had on her math teacher in junior high school, a crush that extended to the man's wife, children and cat.

A great day.

But now it was coming to an end and reality, in one form or another, was waiting to meet them.

He pulled into the parking lot of the bar where they had met the night before. She opened her eyes uncertainly, stifling a yawn, looking around to orient herself. She gave him a quick beautiful smile and kissed his cheek.

"My love," she whispered lightly.

He wanted to turn around, to keep on going in a northerly direction until they reached San Francisco and the safety of his familiar surroundings. But he knew she would not run away from what lay ahead.

"I thought you'd better pick up your car," he said.

Her smile faded. She straightened in the seat, pushing absently at her hair. She said, "The day is over."

"And now you're sure you want to see him alone?"

"We went through that, darling." She laughed good-naturedly. "I think that's the first time I've called you that. Like it?"

"I love it."

She cupped his face in her palm. "Don't worry, Kevin," she said. "Please don't worry. Everything will be fine."

"I know," he said.

"This has to be done."

He nodded.

"After tonight—tonight is the last time, my darling," she said. "I'll tell him and then we'll always be together."

"There's all the red tape of going through a divorce," he said. "I'm not sure I can wait that long, Lili. I want you now, this moment. I want you with me every possible second of the day."

They had talked it over during the day and decided it would be best if she went to Reno for her divorce. Six weeks. Six long, interminable weeks. So damned long. "Are you sure he'll agree?" Kevin had asked.

"He has nothing to say about it," she had assured him. "I'm going to get a divorce, regardless of how he feels. I certainly have the grounds. You said yourself there isn't a court in the country that wouldn't grant me one."

In daylight, their plans had seemed foolproof. Tonight, Kevin felt that something could go wrong. Jim was capable of illogical action.

"Kiss me," she whispered tautly. "Just once. Then I'll go."

Her lips met his, and then suddenly she was out of his arms. He sat alone, trying not to anticipate disaster.

He drove slowly, deliberately keeping his speed down. He was afraid that if he got back too soon, he would be unable to keep his promise to let Lili see her husband alone.

He turned off on the side road and remembered the first time he had seen her, how close he had come to running her down. He even smiled a little, recalling

149

her anger. When she was angry, her eyes sparkled.

The parking lot had space to spare. He got out of his car and stood for a moment in thought, running his hand over the stubble on his face. He would shower and shave and change clothes and, by that time, she should have told Jim the score. He could go to her.

As he walked along the path toward his cabin, he saw Sheri. She was standing in front of her cabin, her luggage on the stoop, talking in a low voice to a man in a brown suit. She turned and looked at Kevin as he passed. There was a change in her, he thought. He gave her companion a second look. The man was tall, dark, and thin, with sharp features.

Sheri asked, "Where's Lili?"

"How would I know?" Kevin replied.

"Don't play games with me, sweetie," she said. "I know how it is between you two. I ought to know."

Kevin nodded at her friend. "I see you've changed your mind again," he said.

"For the better this time." She made no effort at introductions. "Look, sweetie, just because I enjoyed playing tennis with you, I'm going to give you some free advice. Take it or leave it. If Lili's alone with that big bull of a husband of hers, I wouldn't like to see her when he gets done with her. The last time I saw him, he wasn't in a pretty mood."

Kevin felt the shock in a series of little jolts. He did not wait to hear what else she was saying. He turned and started running, hoping he would be in time.

Just this one last hurdle, Lili thought. She would tell Jim how things were, she would be calm and matter-of-fact about it, and then she would pack her things. She kept reminding herself, as she walked towards the cabin, how simple it would be.

Perhaps he would not even be there. Perhaps he would still be with Sheri.

The cabin was dark, the door slightly ajar. She went in, felt for the light switch along the wall. The room was flooded with sudden light and she paused to adjust her vision.

Jim stood at the foot of the bed, looking enormous and somehow blurred, perhaps because he was less than steady on his feet. His hands were shoved in the pockets of his slacks. She felt a familiar tremor of fright.

"Do I worry you, Lili?" he asked.

"I didn't—the lights were out," she stammered. "I didn't think you were here."

"And where would I be, if I weren't here?"

"I don't know." She wondered if her knees were actually shaking or if she only imagined they were. Why should she be so frightened of him? They had lived together as man and wife. He was not a natural force, like a tornado—or was he? "I thought—well, maybe you'd gone to dinner—or something." What was the matter with her?

"It's a little late for dinner, isn't it?"

"Well, I—" She took another step into the room. She could not let him frighten her into mindlessness.

"And where have you been?" he asked.

"I spent the day in Los Angeles."

"And last night? Where did you spend last night?" She braced herself. "In a motel."

"Alone?" There was something insane about his eyes.

"Do you want me to answer that, Jim?"

"You just did." His smile was grim, death-like. "Where is he? Isn't he man enough to come back here with you?"

She bristled, sudden anger displacing the fear. "He's more of a man than you'll ever be, Jim. He knows what being a man is. He—"

"Shut up, damn you," he yelled.

She had not returned to shut up. "I came back to get my things, Jim. I'm leaving you tonight. I'm going to pick up my bags and walk out. I'm going to get a divorce. From now on, you can do what you want, chase after as many little sluts as you wish. I don't care. I'm finished. It's all over between us, Jim."

His laughter was barely a human sound. "You're a riot, Lili," he said. "A real riot."

She frowned. "All right—laugh. But I'm serious."

"What do you want me to do? You want me to get down on my knees and beg you to stay?"

"I don't want anything from you, Jim, not one thing. I just want out."

His strange laughter came again. "You think I'm going to let you divorce me? You think I'm—"

"You've got nothing to say about it," she told him with more briskness than she felt. "I've got plenty of grounds, more than enough. Everyone at home knows that you spend every waking moment chasing anything in skirts. I won't have any trouble getting a divorce, Jim, not one little bit of trouble. Your friends—" she laughed bitterly— "they all laugh behind your back. They know what you are, Jim. It took me a long time to admit the truth to myself, but I do now."

"You lie," he shouted. "No one laughs at me."

"They all do, Jim. Maybe you didn't know it, but they do, every one of them."

"You lie," he shouted again, taking a step toward her, raising his hand menacingly.

From nowhere, a sense of courage came to her. She was not going to break and run. She was going to stand up to him this time, let him know exactly what

152

she thought of him. Looking at him, she felt a twinge of pity. He was lost in his own vicious little world and probably he was lonely.

"I'm sorry, Jim." She tried not to look into his eyes, embarrassed for him. "We're both sensible adults. Let's face the fact that our marriage is a failure and try not to be bitter."

"And if I do give you a divorce, what then?" His voice was strangely calm.

"What difference does it make? We'll go our own ways."

"You'll go to him?"

She forced herself to be honest. "Yes," she said.

He made a strange sound in his throat and grabbed her roughly, pinning her arms to her sides. She had no chance to defend herself as he forced her to the bed. He laughed.

"Jim," she shouted. "No, Jim."

"I'm going to show you what kind of man I am. I'm going to have you like you've never been had before, and then we'll see if you want to leave me. No woman makes a fool out of me."

She struggled vainly to free herself. He bent her back on the bed. His lips bruised her face and neck and she realized that he meant to rape her.

She kicked out in panic. He let out a banshee sound of pain, his hold on her loosening as he stepped back. She ran for the door.

It seemed to her that the door would never open, that she stood for an eternity, twisting the knob. As the door swung open, Jim's hands closed on her sweater. The sweater ripped. She escaped.

In panic, she turned the wrong way, ran wildly toward the beach. She could hear Jim behind her. She stumbled when she came to the turn in the path, fell to her knees and rolled down-hill. She wanted desperately to scream but no sound came from her lips.

She looked up and saw his shape outlined in the shadows. He was making strange noises and reaching for her.

Kevin saw the splash of light from the doorway of her cabin, saw Lili running with Jim close behind her. He yelled her name. He could tell she had not heard him. She was running toward the beach. Jim was gaining on her.

He took after them, angry at himself for letting her see Jim alone, frightened at the thought of losing her.

He reached the hill that overlooked the beach. In the darkness below, he could make out Lili lying on the sand. Jim stood above her, arms outstretched. Kevin yelled, took two long strides and flung himself against the bigger man. They fell to the sand together, a tangle of arms and legs.

Most of the fight would never be clear in Kevin's mind. Some kind of light went on for him when he found himself using a judo punch at the other man's throat. Slowly, very slowly, the big man's fingers loosened their grip on Kevin's neck.

Kevin heard himself gasp for breath. He crawled to his hands and knees. Jim lay on his back a foot or so away.

He heard Lili whisper his name. He managed to get to his feet. There was a dull throbbing in his head and his throat felt raw. He swayed uncertainly.

Lili came to him, like a lost child. She sobbed. "I thought I could do it alone. But I'm no good alone any more. I need you, I need you—" He buried his face in her hair, smelling the sweet scent of her, knowing that everything was going to be all right now.

THE END

154

Other BEACON-SIGNAL BOOKS to Enjoy!

If you've enjoyed this book; we know you will want to read the many other BEACON-SIGNAL BOOKS now available for your reading pleasure.

You will find them as stimulating, pulse-quickening and invigorating a collection of novels as you could run across in a month of Sundays. These books are fiery, red-blooded, full of exciting, passionate adventure, calculated to give you hours of fascination.

Note the titles and capsule descriptions listed below and on the following pages . . . jot down your selections on the coupon provided for your convenience . . . and get set for real tingling reading enjoyment!

And . . . the more books you select the lower the price becomes. We pay the postage.

Order today, while we still have all the titles in stock!

B-527 **THE MARRIAGE BED** by Laura Hale
Gripping story of a woman trapped by a marriage so warped that
it stripped her of all decency.

B-528 **NEST OF SUMMER WIDOWS** by Francis Loren
A startling revelation of how restless women fill their days—and
nights!

B-529 **THE DECEIVERS** by L. T. Woodward, M.D.
Sexual misbehavior among suburban couples—from a doctor's
personal casebook!

B-530 **BEDROOMS ON WHEELS** by Brian O'Bannon
Construction men and their young, restless women sit on a powder
keg of sex.

TAKE ADVANTAGE OF OUR SPECIAL LOW PRICES
MAIL-ORDER BLANK TODAY!

**ALL BOOKS ARE 50¢ EACH. IF YOU ORDER MORE THAN 4,
YOU GET FREE BOOKS OF YOUR OWN CHOICE!**

1 to 4 Books—Enclose a 5¢ additional handling charge for each book. (In
case we're out of stock, list two substitute titles on the coupon.)
5 to 8 Books—You get 1 book free. Indicate which free title you want on
the back of this form. (List four substitute titles.)
9 to 12 Books—You get 2 books free. (List 6 substitute titles.)
13 or more Books—You get 3 books free. (List 8 substitute titles.)

BEACON-SIGNAL BOOKS, P.O. Box 2080
Grand Central Station, New York 17, N. Y.

Please send me the books encircled below. I enclose.............

B-445	B-459	B-471	B-485	B-497	B-509	B-521
B-446	B-460	B-472	B-486	B-498	B-510	B-522
B-448	B-461	B-473	B-487	B-499	B-511	B-523
B-449	B-462	B-474	B-488	B-500	B-512	B-524
B-450	B-463	B-475	B-489	B-501	B-513	B-525
B-452	B-464	B-476	B-490	B-502	B-514	B-526
B-453	B-465	B-477	B-491	B-503	B-515	B-527
B-454	B-466	B-478	B-492	B-504	B-516	B-528
B-455	B-467	B-479	B-493	B-505	B-517	B-529
B-456	B-468	B-480	B-494	B-506	B-518	B-530
B-457	B-469	B-481	B-495	B-507	B-519	
B-458	B-470	B-482	B-496	B-508	B-520	

In the event we are out of stock on any of your selections, please list
your alternative choices:

1............ 2............ 3............ 4............

5............ 6............ 7............ 8............

NAME ....

ADDRESS ....

CITY.................. ZONE..... STATE............